"Your place or mine?"

he asked impudently and then laughed at the expression on her face. He helped her from the Jeep and walked with her to the front door.

"Since the evening was such a success, why don't we do it again tomorrow night?" he suggested brazenly.

"As I said earlier, Mr. Savage, this was our *last* date."

"Then as *I* said earlier, I'd better make the most of it."

Without warning, his hands gripped her shoulders, and he pulled her to him. Then, in complete contrast to the rough, urgent movement, his lips descended on hers in a kiss so gentle and soft that it left her wondering if he had kissed her at all. Shaken, she took a step backward until she felt the support of the front door against her back.

"Someone should have told you, Mr. Savage, when you bought us out, that I do not come with the property."

Dear Reader:

After more than one year of publication, SECOND CHANCE AT LOVE has a lot to celebrate. Not only has it become firmly established as a major line of paperback romances, but response from our readers also continues to be warm and enthusiastic. Your letters keep pouring in—and we love receiving them. We're getting to know you—your likes and dislikes—and want to assure you that your contribution does make a difference.

As we work hard to offer you better and better SECOND CHANCE AT LOVE romances, we're especially gratified to hear that you, the reader, are rating us higher and higher. After all, our success depends on *you*. We're pleased that you enjoy our books and that you appreciate the extra effort our writers and staff put into them. Thanks for spreading the good word about SECOND CHANCE AT LOVE and for giving us your loyal support. Please keep your suggestions and comments coming!

With warm wishes,

Ellen Edwards

Ellen Edwards
SECOND CHANCE AT LOVE
The Berkley/Jove Publishing Group
200 Madison Avenue
New York, NY 10016

Second Chance at Love

BEYOND PRIDE
KATHLEEN ASH

A SECOND CHANCE AT LOVE BOOK

BEYOND PRIDE

Copyright © 1982 by Kathleen Ash

Distributed by Berkley/Jove

All rights reserved. No part of this publication may be reproduced or transmitted in any form or by any means, electronic or mechanical, including photocopy, recording, or any information storage and retrieval system, without permission in writing from the publisher.

Requests for permission to make copies of any part of the work should be mailed to: Permissions, Second Chance at Love, The Berkley/Jove Publishing Group, 200 Madison Avenue, New York, NY 10016.

First edition published October 1982

First printing

"Second Chance at Love" and the butterfly emblem are trademarks belonging to Jove Publications, Inc.

Printed in the United States of America

Second Chance at Love books are published by
The Berkley/Jove Publishing Group
200 Madison Avenue, New York, NY 10016

chapter 1

THE CAR EMITTED unhealthy choking gasps and shuddered feverishly up a steep incline.

"Damn the old wreck," Jessica muttered between clenched teeth. Promptly the car came to an offended halt and refused to budge again. Jessica slammed a fist down on the steering wheel in helpless frustration.

Among the Romney possessions that had had to be disposed of after their financial ruin had been the family's fleet of cars. Faced with the choice of keeping just one, Jessica Romney had wanted the rugged, practical station wagon that had been used for estate business. But Carlotta and Iris had pleaded for one of the more stately cars. Since Jessica's mother-in-law and sister-in-law had been stripped of most of the luxurious trappings of their lives by their recent calamity, Jessica had relented and finally decided upon the smaller of the family's limousines, which, after almost thirty years of service, truly qualified as a vintage piece.

But, as Jessica now contemplated furiously, while a car like this might be a collector's dream, it was proving to be nothing but a nightmare to her. It required highly specialized care to keep it in good working order, something that the tiny local garage was unable to provide, and the cost of which was a great strain on Jessica's strict new budget.

She got out and gave the car a savage glare. Jessica could not easily tolerate a situation in which she was helpless, but in the matter of broken-down cars she had to admit defeat. She fought back the tears that so easily threatened these days. She who never, never cried. At least there was comfort in the thought that she had rarely allowed them to fall in the fifteen months since her husband's death. Most people would have readily excused the tears of a young widow, who had had to face not only death but also almost complete financial ruin. And, worst of all, this humiliation had happened to a family that had been local royalty for generations in this part of Australia.

But Jessica allowed herself no such excuses. She despised and fought every inclination to weakness. She looked around her now but saw no one. It wasn't far to Sommerville and home, just far enough to make the walk back on the rocky and hilly backroad a nuisance. There wasn't much chance of getting any help here, either. It wasn't a much frequented way into town. She let out a deep sigh of frustration and leaned her slim, tall body against the front fender while she searched for a solution. Her vivid green eyes narrowed as she looked in the distance toward Sommerville. At least the ordeal of selling Romney House was behind her, and she and Carlotta and Iris were settled into their new home. So let that rich intruder—what was his name? Savage, Peter Savage— take possession of his new acquisition and see how at home he felt in a place that had been built for Romneys and had always been lived in by Romneys.

For a moment a derisive smile touched Jessica's face. How comical that she should think of someone else as an outsider when she was not only an outsider herself but a foreigner besides. Five years ago she had come as a new bride from South Carolina to this exclusive little farming district in southwest New South Wales, only three hours' drive from Sydney. It was populated mostly by gentlemen farmers whose properties, passed on from generation to generation, looked more like landscaped showplaces than real farms. The community was not given to opening its arms wide to strangers. Jessica had been treated differently because she had come as a Romney. As for Mr. Savage...as always, the thought of him spurred her to unreasonable resentment.

"Damn you!" she said aloud, giving one of the tires a vicious kick.

"That's no way to treat a grand old lady. Don't you have any respect for age?" a man's deep voice said not ten feet away from her.

Startled, Jessica jumped. A moment ago when she had looked about she'd seen no one. He must have been hidden in the small ravine by the side of the road. How long had he been standing there watching her struggle with the car?

Annoyed at having been caught in the middle of a temper tantrum, she answered in a none-too-friendly tone. "Grand old lady, indeed! More like a senile old thing. Gives me no end of trouble."

The man had come closer and was studying the car with open admiration. "That's a real beauty, a great-looking old Bentley. What year—'55, '56?"

"I really have no idea," Jessica said testily, in no mood to chat with a vintage-car nut. The least he could do was offer some help. "It's just a troublesome wreck to me."

The man looked at her closely for the first time, his expression making it clear that she had not only said something irreverent but also stupid. He turned back to the car, studying it closely.

Meanwhile, Jessica studied him. He was very big, with coarse blond hair carelessly cut and skin burnt a reddish-brown. He was somewhere in his mid-thirties, probably a laborer of some sort, Jessica decided, glancing at his worn, dust-covered jeans, faded shirt, sturdy workman's boots, and powerful, work-roughened hands, in which he was holding a piece of rock.

"Do you happen to know anything about cars?" she ventured hopefully.

The man transferred his attention from the car to Jessica. Slowly and deliberately his bright blue eyes moved down her body, from her long golden-brown hair to her slender neck, her full breasts, slim waist, rounded hips, and long legs. His eyes returned to her breasts and lingered boldly. He nodded briefly.

Jessica checked her rising temper. "Then would you mind looking at this one to see if you can get it started?" she asked as if speaking to a slow-witted child.

He kept his eyes on her a moment longer, then shrugged. "Okay. But promise not to kick me if I can't. Hold this," he commanded, handing her the rock.

Jessica took it gingerly and caught the hint of a smile as he turned from her toward the car. Was he making a fool of her? Her green eyes narrowed as she looked at him.

For the next ten minutes he seemed to be absorbed in his work under the hood. He ignored her completely—a situation to which Jessica was unaccustomed. She felt a sudden and perverse dislike for this man. He hadn't said anything rude, but there was something in his manner, something that suggested he had sized her up and was amused by what he had seen. She almost wished he wouldn't be able to fix the car.

Almost at once he straightened up and turned to her. "That should do it," he said, and he got in and turned the ignition. The car gave a gentle, obedient purr. He got out and stood aside for her.

"Thank you *so* much," Jessica said just a little too sweetly.

He nodded in acknowledgment. "You ought to take better care of her. A magnificent machine like that shouldn't be neglected. If you don't have her seen to, she'll break down again. Next time I might not be around." Jessica wasn't quite sure if there was a smile on his face or not.

"That *would* be awful," she said, resentful of the lecture.

This time there was no mistaking the grin. As she looked closely at him, she noticed that his nose was slightly irregular as if it had once been broken. The thought gave her some satisfaction; then immediately she was appalled at herself. Now what had made her react like that to a man who had helped her? she wondered.

The man was returning her look evenly. "What's a Yank girl like you doing in this part of the world?" he asked. "Are you a tourist?"

Being called a Yank always set Jessica's teeth on edge. First, she hated hearing the term applied to any American, and second, she was a Southerner.

"I'm not a Yank girl. I'm an American from South Carolina. Ever hear of the place?" she asked nastily.

"Yes, ma'am. Sure 'nuff have," he replied in imitation of a servant.

Jessica flushed and turned to get into the car, then remembered that she was still holding the rock.

"Good heavens, I almost made off with your stone," she said in exaggerated alarm, placing it into his hands with the greatest of care. "Is rock collecting your hobby, or do you do it for a living?" she asked sarcastically.

"It's not just a rock, it's a sample of sandstone," he said matter-of-factly, ignoring her tone. "If you were from these parts you'd know that. This area used to provide the best veined sandstone in New South Wales. Most of the buildings around here are built from it."

"Oh well, I know less about rocks than I do about vintage cars." She knew she was being rude but couldn't seem to help herself. She got into the car.

The man stooped down and leaned in the window. "And yes, I do it for a living," he said, looking at her so intently and for so long that, to her horror, she felt herself flushing.

"Then you're not a car mechanic?" she asked, just to say something.

"No. I'm in the building trade."

She turned the ignition. "Thank you for your help."

Without a word he backed away and turned to go. Jessica felt annoyance rising in her. She hated the way she had come off in this encounter. The man had actually managed to fluster her! If she didn't put him in his place, this meeting would remain unsatisfactorily incomplete for her.

"Young man," she called after him, sounding to her own ears like her mother-in-law at her most imperious.

He turned at once and strolled back to the car.

"Ma'am?" His voice had taken on the mock servility again.

"If you're a builder and happen to be looking for work, I might have some for you. It might pay a little better than rock collecting."

He looked at her questioningly.

"Can you mend a roof?"

"Yes, ma'am."

"Any good at carpentry? Could you build some bookshelves?"

"I think so... ma'am."

"In that case," Jessica said, borrowing Carlotta Romney's most condescending manner, "I might be able to give you some odd jobs. I'll write down the address. Ask for Mrs. Romney."

The look of surprise on his face was unmistakable. So, she thought with satisfaction, he knows the name. Tourist indeed! Before he could reply, she stepped hard on the gas pedal and drove off.

Jessica stepped back from the shelves and surveyed her work critically. How to cram as many of the several thousand volumes from the library of Romney House onto the inadequate shelves of this small study was indeed a problem. The books, a rare and extensive collection put together by four generations of Romneys, was one of the few things Jessica had refused to sell. While she had watched with composure as paintings, furniture, rugs, china, and silver vanished under the auctioneer's hammer, she had not been able to let the books go. Her husband Roderick had treasured them.

They stood now in packing cases all over the house, and Jessica had to make room for them—only one of many problems she'd confronted since they'd moved from the thirty-room Romney mansion into this eight-room cottage.

As she stooped to pick up another pile of books, the door burst open and Iris Romney rushed into the room. She paused at its exact center before announcing dramatically, "Well, they're here! They have *descended!*"

"Descended?" Jessica glanced at her sister-in-law with amusement. "You make them sound like a plague of locusts."

"*Very* similar," Iris said with an emphatic toss of her head.

"Let me guess. You're talking about the new owner of Romney House?"

"Who else?" Iris said, abandoning her dramatic tone in a rush of excited words. "I hear he has sent ahead five giant furniture vans and—"

"Who has?" a plaintive voice inquired from the doorway. Carlotta Romney made her languid way into the room, wearing a much ruffled peach negligee.

As she entered, Jessica mused on how Iris and Carlotta were exactly alike—or at least as alike as two women separated by twenty-five years could be. Both had vivid red hair, luminously white skin, and sapphire-blue eyes, a tendency toward plumpness, and a penchant for the dramatic in both dress and manner.

Carlotta sank wearily into a deep armchair. "Iris, *must* you be so noisy at this hour of the morning?" she complained to her daughter.

"It's almost eleven o'clock, Mother," Iris said in automatic contradiction before going on excitedly. "I was just telling Jessica that he has sent five vans and—"

"Who has?" Carlotta interrupted again.

"Oh, Mother." Iris turned on her impatiently. "You know very well I'm talking about that Mr. What's-his-name."

"Savage," Jessica volunteered, though she knew her sister-in-law's forgetfulness was only a pretense. The man's name was engraved indelibly on all their memories.

"That dreadful man!" Carlotta said, her hands raised as if to ward off some horror.

"Carlotta, we don't even know him," Jessica protested, even though she shared the same prejudice against the new owner.

"I know all I want to," Carlotta said with uncharacteristic energy. "He has put us out of our home. The home of my ancestors." A dainty square of linen and lace stifled a rising sob.

"The home of *my* ancestors you mean, don't you?" Iris, always ready to squabble with her mother, demanded. "Remember, you're only a Romney by marriage, whereas I was born—"

"Someone had to buy the place," Jessica cut in, forestalling an inevitable argument between the two women. She was not so much defending the new owner as she was trying to calm Iris and Carlotta. "We had to sell, and this man bought it. You can hardly claim that he deliberately put us out of—"

"To be reduced to this... this hovel," Carlotta sobbed on unheeding, waving a tragic hand around the small but attractive room.

"Millions of people would not consider an eight-room house surrounded by a half acre of land exactly a hovel," Jessica pointed out mildly.

"They are not Romneys!" Carlotta said, squelching the argument with majesty.

Jessica regarded the two women, and not for the first time in the fifteen months of her widowhood felt the heavy burden of responsibility that had descended on her with her husband's death.

The only family left to her were these two women, who had been so indulged and protected all their lives that they were still unable to comprehend the reality of what had befallen them. Though Jessica came from the other side of the world, her background was not so very different from theirs. But unlike them, she had been brought up to face the realities of life. After all, she came from the South, where facing and surviving calamities gracefully had been bred into families for generations.

But no such example had ever served the other two women. No part of Australia had ever been invaded—at least not in the two-hundred-year history of its white settlement. Certainly very few families in this lush, wealthy pocket of New South Wales had ever faced ruin. It had taken the Romneys themselves generations of indifference to financial management to have arrived at this disastrous point.

Carlotta had been one of that now vanished breed, the debutante, who had been presented at court in London just before that stuffy custom was finally abandoned. She had come to Romney House as a young bride and had never had the energy or interest to seek anything outside her own pampered family circle.

Iris too had gone to London while still in her teens, not for her debut as her mother had done, but to do what was fashionable with her generation—to make a career. Briefly she had tried acting and marriage and given up both as requiring too much effort. Since then she too had lived in luxurious isolation.

Jessica had been a Romney for only five years, but now in misfortune she felt as fiercely protective toward the family as if she had been a member for generations. She had come to Australia a month after her wedding, had been welcomed with open arms, had shared the best with the Romneys, and was now determined to share the worst. It had never occurred to her to go back to the United States.

With Roderick's death, what for many years had been a troublesome small cloud on the horizon had suddenly turned black and become a deluge. There was no money left, only a formidable pile of debts.

Jessica had found herself in charge of two helpless women with a proud family name to uphold. She had made calm plans in the midst of disaster. She had seen to the disposal of the beloved home they could no longer afford, had sold and leased out land, and arranged for the family to move to a smaller house a quarter mile away. She had calculated their future survival down to the last detail. It was Jessica, too, who had insisted that they stay in Sommerville and see the thing through with their heads held high. Plenty of people would enjoy the spectacle of watching the mighty fall, but she would not give them the satisfaction of seeing them flee. To Jessica pride and courage counted above all else, and in the past fifteen months she had drawn heavily on her own reserves of these qualities to keep the last three Romneys going.

To a large extent this responsibility had helped her to survive her own grief. Now Jessica looked at the two women with sincere affection.

"I bet he fits his name," Iris said ominously.

"What?" Jessica asked.

"Savage! Don't you get it? I bet the man *is* a bloody savage," Iris explained, delighted with her observation.

"Don't be coarse, dear," Carlotta said absently and shuddered at an idea of her own. "Five vans of furniture, did you say? I can just imagine what sort of furniture, too. Nasty, tasteless stuff. When I think of all the beautiful pieces that were in our family for years..." The words were drowned in a fresh torrent of tears.

Jessica put a comforting arm around her mother-in-law. Secretly she shared her feelings. She too was filled with horror at the thought of what an intruder might do to the beautiful, stately rooms of Romney House. For try as she would, she could think of the new owner in no other way. She too nursed an unreasonable resentment toward him.

With the irrelevance that was typical of her, Iris now said, "Do you suppose we ought to call on him?"

At her mother's astonished look, she added defiantly, "I believe it *is* the polite thing to call on a new neighbor. Am I wrong? Just because we have lost everything else, we haven't lost our manners too, I hope?"

"Fortunately, calling on people is no longer a social obligation," Jessica said. "There are some compensations for the loss of social graces today. Minding one's own business is one of the better ones."

Iris, who found minding her own business a boring pastime, insisted, "But we live practically next door. It's inevitable that we meet him sooner or later."

"Later will be quite soon enough," Jessica insisted.

"And *never* will be too soon for *me*," Carlotta sniffed. She rose from her armchair and patted Jessica on the arm. "You're getting too thin, dear. You're working too hard," she said, looking at Jessica's slim, tall figure. Carlotta could still not accept that the vogue for voluptuous women had been over for many years.

"I wish someone would say that to me just once." Iris sighed enviously, patting her own rounded hips. "Come on, Mother. I'll do your hair in that new style."

The two women left, and Jessica turned back to the task of arranging books. What they needed were more shelves. That entire wall could be covered with shelves without destroying the proportion of the room.

Her thoughts returned to her encounter the day before with the stranger whom she had hired in such a high-handed way. The memory of her behavior made her wince with embarrassment. What had made her act that way? Thank heavens she would never have to face him again. She was quite certain he wouldn't turn up for the job. She tried to put the incident out of her mind, but she felt as if his bold blue eyes were still assessing her.

chapter 2

JESSICA WAS ELBOW deep in soil, kneeling in a small round flower bed she had dug over the past couple of days.

It was an already warm morning of what promised to be a hot October day in the Australian spring. She felt a deep satisfaction in the work, which was a complete novelty for her. Her experience in gardening had not extended beyond snipping off flowers for the dozens of arrangements that had adorned Romney House. She tried to remember some of the tasks Mr. Curtis, the regular gardener there, had done, but mostly she relied on instinct.

The grounds of the cottage rambled haphazardly, and she had already decided that she would attempt little besides improving the lawn and weeding and pruning the garden. It was not the sort of garden you could force into order. That would have destroyed its charm. She liked the way the native trees, bushes, and plants ran riot with a will of their own. She would leave them as they were and plant only some of her favorites in special flower beds—like roses, daffodils, hyacinths, and lilies of the valley.

On this spring morning the garden was already stirring to life. The lavender bushes were in bloom, and a half-dozen pink and white azalea bushes were coming into their full glory. Jessica surveyed the wide variety of plants—two giant native ghost gum trees, a wattle tree, hibiscus bushes with enormous red and pink flowers, frangipani trees, bushes of creeping fragrant jasmine, magnolias, gardenias, and several jacaranda trees, whose heavy purple flower clusters were among the most beautiful sights of an Australian summer. Yes, she would let the garden follow its own will. She preferred it to sweeping lawns and flower beds laid out with rigid formality.

She stood up and wiped her hands absently on her tan shorts, leaving a wide streak of dirt on either side. Her faded red T-shirt was soiled too, and her slim bare legs, already tanned from having spent several sunny days in the garden, were caked with mud at the knees.

She looked about her and breathed deeply of the fresh, clear air. Mornings like this compensated for a lot of the problems in life, she thought gratefully. Earlier a kookaburra family had put in an appearance, serenading her with their chorus of infectious laughter. They had ventured quite close when she'd brought some scraps from the kitchen for them. She hoped they were nesting nearby and would become frequent visitors. After five years in the country she still felt a thrill at the sight and sound of Australia's most beloved birds.

Jessica felt the soil clinging grittily inside one sneaker and reached down to take it off. She drew up one leg, balancing herself awkwardly on the other, and had just begun to remove the shoe when she lost her balance and almost fell over. Before she could regain her footing, a strong, steadying hand gripped her arm.

She whirled around and faced the man she had met on the road two days before. The shock of seeing him so unexpectedly paralyzed her for a moment, and she remained standing as he continued to hold her, staring up at him. She hadn't heard him approach and was embarrassed to have been startled by him a second time. As she stared into his blue eyes, only inches from her own, she realized with surprise just how often she had thought of him in the past two days.

"Steady," he murmured, a slow smile lighting his face.

Beyond Pride

"What are you doing here?" Jessica asked faintly, still reeling from surprise.

"Reporting for work, as you asked me to do," he replied as matter-of-factly as if the few words they had exchanged two days before had been a binding contract. When she said nothing, he asked, "Or have you changed your mind? Don't you have any work for me to do?"

"Well... yes," Jessica began hesitantly, then realized how foolish she sounded and added more decisively, "Of course I do, or I wouldn't have offered the job to you." She managed to sound businesslike enough, but in truth did not know what to do now that he *was* here. She had never for a moment expected him to come. Only now did she notice that he was still holding her by the arm. She looked pointedly down at his hand. His eyes followed her glance and he removed his hand unhurriedly. Then his eyes traveled further down to take in her bare, soiled legs and make a detailed journey up again until they reached her face.

Jessica stood silently under his appraisal, seething with anger and embarrassment. This wasn't the first time he had given her such a brazen once-over, and she would not tolerate it. She raised her chin defiantly and regarded him with a cool, disdainful expression, refusing to reveal how acutely conscious she was of her grubby appearance.

She wanted to fire him on the spot, but the fact that she didn't like the way he was looking at her legs didn't seem a very good reason. Recovering her equanimity with some effort, she decided to cover up the fact that she had hired him purely on impulse, never expecting him to show up. After all, the roof *did* need fixing and the shelves had to be built, and since he was here, he might as well do the work. But before she could give him instructions, he took matters into his own hands.

"That the roof that needs fixing?" he asked, nodding toward the cottage.

"Yes. It leaks in a couple of places."

He stood silently inspecting the two-story sandstone cottage built in the Australian colonial style 150 years before. It had a wide sloping roof and deep verandas on three sides to shelter it from the fierce summer heat. The cottage was graceful in its simplicity and lack of adornment and had a look of sturdiness, as if it was ready to take on the coming centuries. It had been built to accommodate the succession of property managers who had served the Romney estates over the years. For a while now it had been untenanted and neglected.

"It's a beauty," the stranger finally said with admiration. "They don't know how to build houses like this anymore. That sandstone will withstand anything."

Jessica looked at the house through new eyes. To the Romneys, coming here from their vast and imposing mansion with their few remaining possessions meant a falling on hard times. But she realized that to most people owning an authentic colonial sandstone cottage like this one represented a fulfillment of the great Australian dream.

"I'll have to get up to the roof to have a look. Got a ladder somewhere?" the man asked, interrupting Jessica's thoughts.

"I think there's one in that small shed over there," she told him, pointing to a corner of the garden. "I don't know if it's long enough."

"I'll have a look." He sauntered away from her. Jessica stood there, slightly dazed. Involuntarily her hand went to her elbow. She could still feel the heat of his rough hand. She remembered the way he had looked at her and frowned toward the shed into which he had disappeared. How had she gotten herself into this mess, anyway? Well, she'd get herself out soon enough. As soon as he finished the job she'd pay him and that would be that.

Several minutes later he returned, carrying a ladder.

"Will it be long enough?" Jessica asked.

"It will do," he replied. "I looked around while I was in there and found some stacks of the slate tiles you have on the roof now. Perhaps there are enough to replace the broken ones." He squinted toward the house. "As far as

I can tell from down here, it shouldn't be a big job. But I'll have to climb up on the roof to see. You'll have to show me the trapdoor in the ceiling where I can get up."

Jessica led the way into the cottage through a wide hall that divided the house from front door to back. Rooms opened onto it on either side. A small staircase on the left led to the upper floor, where the bedrooms were. Jessica led him up the stairs and paused uncertainly, realizing suddenly that she had no idea what a ceiling trapdoor was or if the house even had one.

Fortunately the stranger's expert eye found it at once in a corner of the small upstairs hall. He set up the ladder under it.

"Will you be able to manage?" Jessica asked.

"Yes," he said, barely glancing at her, concentrating on opening the door in the ceiling. For some reason his lack of attention annoyed Jessica as much as his too thorough scrutiny had earlier.

"Well then, I'll leave you to it," she said briskly, receiving no reply. She went into her bedroom and stood at the window before deciding to abandon gardening for the day and take a shower. She glanced into the hall, but he had already disappeared through the opening onto the roof.

She stood under the shower vigorously rubbing her knees and soiled fingernails with a hard brush, all the time aware of the man who was on the roof at that very moment. Once she even glanced nervously at the ceiling to make certain he couldn't look in on her. The thought embarrassed her enough to make her finish her shower quickly and seek shelter in a large bath towel.

After all, she was alone in the house with a complete stranger. Carlotta and Iris had gone visiting the evening before and had stayed up so late playing cards that they'd decided to stay the night and not return until lunchtime. And Mrs. Green, the part-time cleaning woman, wouldn't be coming today. The thought of being alone with the man made Jessica a little uncomfortable, but she knew instinctively that he wasn't a threat in *that* way.

After her shower she dressed in a cool green-and-white-print cotton dress and white sandals, brushed her shoulder-length hair behind her ears, and paused at the dressing table only long enough to dab on some pink lip gloss and add a spray of cologne.

As she went out into the hall, she heard a faint hammering from above. She checked the other bedrooms to see if they were neat and opened the windows wider to let the fresh air in. They no longer had maids to attend to such household needs.

Iris's contribution to their hard times was cooking. In London she had attended cordon bleu cooking classes with other fashionable young women, and now her one great accomplishment in life was cooking. She prepared extravagant meals that ruined their budget, but it was one way in which Jessica could indulge Iris. Their only help was Mrs. Green, who came to clean three days a week. These conditions, Jessica well realized, would not have constituted a hardship for most Australians. People who had to struggle for every dollar would have laughed at what the Romneys called hard times, but for the two pampered women it was a difficult and bitter adjustment.

Jessica spent the next hour in the study making business calls and balancing accounts, tasks at which she had become quite adept. She became so deeply absorbed in the work that it was a while before she realized that the hammering had stopped. She went outside and saw the workman standing a short distance from the house surveying his work.

He saw her and came over. "It's done," he said.

"Already?" she asked with surprise.

"Not much needed doing. Some loose and broken tiles, which I've replaced. One of the supports is a little rickety and should be replaced too, but I'll need timber for that, so it'll have to wait for another day."

"But that's wonderful. I thought it would take much longer and that there would be an awful mess."

"Not when I'm on the job," the stranger said, and he smiled down at her so unexpectedly, so warmly, so lack-

Beyond Pride 19

ing in his usual mockery that for a moment she was caught off guard, and her heart skipped a beat.

"Can I... Would you care for something to drink?" she asked in some confusion.

"Thanks." He nodded. "But first show me where you want those shelves."

Jessica showed him into the study. He dwarfed the small, low-ceilinged room as he stood looking about him. She saw with surprise that he was taking a sincere interest in the ancient rugs, the fine old furniture, the watercolors that covered the walls, the small treasures that covered the desk and tables. He examined everything carefully but made no comment. Instead he pointed to the wall she had already picked out and said, "You could build shelves along that side. The shape of the room could accommodate that."

Jessica agreed with him and privately decided that, with such a feeling for design, he must be more than just a handyman. As he got busy with a retractable tape measure, which he pulled from one of his pockets, she went into the kitchen and poured a tall glass of beer for him, then returned to the study.

He continued measuring and jotting down figures while taking gulps from his drink. "What sort of wood did you have in mind?" he asked.

Jessica hesitated. She couldn't say the cheapest, though that was all she could afford. Instead she said, "Just something very plain. They'll be painted anyway."

He nodded. "I'll order the wood for you in town. I know my way around the local timber yard. When I've got it, I'll come back and build the shelves for you. Shouldn't take more than a couple of days."

"All right," Jessica agreed. "Meanwhile I'd like to pay you for the work you did on the roof." She headed for the desk and her open check book.

"There's no charge."

"What?" Jessica wheeled around in surprise. "Of course there is. I insist," she said.

"Well, if you insist..." he said, making a show of

deliberating on a fair price for his work, "then have dinner with me."

Jessica's brows drew together. "I prefer to do my transactions in money," she told him coldly.

"But I won't take money, so I guess you'll just have to stay in my debt." He shrugged and headed for the door.

The last thing Jessica wanted was to remain in this man's debt. "Just a minute," she called after him. He turned expectantly. "You *must* be paid for your morning's work. Now if you'll just be reasonable and—"

"This is one argument that won't go your way, ma'am," he interrupted. "And the debt remains... unless you condescend to go to dinner with a common laborer like me."

Jessica was stunned. Did he think that was the reason she was turning him down? Was he implying that she was a snob? She took a closer look at his impassive face and realized he meant exactly that.

"Your profession has nothing to do with it," she told him indignantly. "But I don't go out to dinner with men I don't know."

"You've just spent a whole morning alone with me in this house," he pointed out. "Which makes that excuse lamer than a legless duck." His blue eyes challenged her.

"When would you like me to go to dinner with you?" she asked bravely, returning his look.

"Tonight. Seven o'clock."

"Very well."

"Swell," he drawled in a parody of an American accent and turned to the door. But not before Jessica saw a triumphant smirk flash across his face. For a long time after he was gone, she stood furiously contemplating the way in which he'd conned her.

She was finally roused by Iris and Carlotta's return. The two women immediately filled the room with their comments on the card party.

"Jessica," Iris said after a while, "I've been trying to persuade Mother that we should give a teensy little dinner party one night this week. I've got a few gorgeous recipes I've been dying to try out. I thought we could invite half a dozen people—the Cuttlers are in town for the picnic races—you know, just a few close friends. It's really time we emerged from hiding, don't you think?"

"You're probably right," Jessica agreed absently. "I've been thinking we should invite a few people over, too."

"Oh, goody," Iris said excitedly. "Why don't you and I sit down after dinner and plan the whole thing?"

"Not tonight, I'm afraid. I...I have a dinner engagement."

Both women looked at her in astonishment. Jessica never went out at night anymore.

"A dinner engagement? With whom?" Iris asked curiously.

"With a common laborer," Jessica said crossly and stormed out of the room.

"What did she say?" she heard Iris ask her mother.

"Oh dear...I think she said something about a laborer," Carlotta said incredulously. "Do you suppose she means she has met a politician from the Labor party and is dining with him tonight? Our family has always supported the Liberals...."

At 6:30 Jessica reluctantly began to dress for dinner. By then the tumult her announcement had caused in the household had more or less subsided. When Iris and Carlotta had heard the story, or as much of it as she had cared to tell them, Carlotta had almost succumbed to one of her attacks of palpitation. Jessica couldn't help smiling at the memory.

"Really, Jessica, that's carrying economy a little too far," her mother-in-law had gasped. "When it comes to you going out with some plumber to save paying the bill—"

"Not a plumber, Mother, she said a—" Iris had begun.

"Whatever." Carlotta had impatiently waved her daughter to silence. "Jessica darling, how could you!"

Jessica had put an arm around her mother-in-law.

"You act as if I've disgraced the family honor and ruined my reputation. Any minute now I expect you to toss me out into the snow."

Iris's giggle had earned her a searing look from her mother.

"It's nothing terrible, dear," Jessica had continued lightly. "I'm just going to have a quick dinner with a man who has helped us out. I'll thank him very politely afterward and never see him again. All right?"

But it had taken a long time to calm Carlotta down, and it hadn't helped matters when Iris had mused loudly, "What a perfectly wonderful solution for paying all our bills. Let's see, tomorrow I could have lunch with the butcher, and I've run up a little bill at the delicatessen— two dinners should take care of that. As for the milkman, I think we should have an evening out at the local pub. Oh, Mother, for heaven's sake, don't have the vapors!"

Now, a half hour before her date, Jessica stood at her open closet having an unusually hard time deciding what to wear. She couldn't look too grand, but if she dressed down too much she was certain he would notice. Choosing the right clothes had never been a problem for her before, but then she had never had a date like this before, either.

Her closet was very full. The Romney women had always been lavish clothes buyers, shopping in New York, London, and the boutiques of the local designers of Sydney and Melbourne. Between them they had enough exquisite lingerie, day and evening clothes, handmade shoes, and purses to see them through several lean years. Jessica rifled through the tightly packed closet, rejecting one dress after another. That deceptively simple-looking black sheath was a little too sophisticated. The pale green would not do; it was backless. The red chiffon was a little low-necked.

Finally she settled on the plainest evening outfit she owned, a butter-yellow silk dress and jacket that was simple yet stylish enough for any setting. With it she wore only a small pair of pearl-and-diamond earrings,

Beyond Pride

a small string of pearls, and her wedding and engagement rings. As she looked down at the diamonds on her finger, she realized with a twist of her heart that this was the first time she was going out with another man since she had met Roderick six years before.

She was just putting the finishing touches to her makeup when the doorbell rang.

"Blast!" she exploded. She had meant to be down in time to answer it. Confronting the formidable duo of Iris and Carlotta for the first time might prove a little too much for even this self-assured man. She raced for the door, but a sudden painful constriction of her stomach made her slow down. She realized with horror that she was very, very nervous.

She was beaten to the front door, but at least it was by Iris, not Carlotta. Iris held the door open while she looked the tall stranger over with frank admiration.

Jessica's own eyes widened a little as she caught sight of him. He was dressed in a beautifully cut gray flannel jacket with darker gray slacks and a dazzlingly laundered white shirt. His fair hair was smoothly brushed, and he looked perfectly groomed from head to toe without giving the effect of being dressed up, as so many men did when they changed from their everyday clothes. He looked natural and at ease. The clothes had been unmistakably tailor-made for him.

Jessica hoped she had effectively covered her surprise as she prepared to introduce him to Iris. But at that moment Carlotta emerged from the drawing room wearing the expression Marie Antoinette must have sported when she went to meet her executioners. At the sight of the well-dressed, attractive visitor, her expression underwent a perceptible change.

"Carlotta, Iris, this is Mr...." With sickening embarrassment Jessica realized she didn't know his name.

Unperturbed by the awkward pause, he turned to the two women and smiled politely. "How do you do? I'm Peter Savage."

chapter 3

STUNNED SILENCE FILLED the room. For the first time since Jessica had known them, Carlotta and Iris were speechless. If Peter Savage noticed the explosion his little bomb had caused, he showed no sign of it. He appeared perfectly at ease while he looked about the room, as if tactfully giving the women time to recover.

Then everything began to move again in slow motion. Everyone was talking politely, if a little stiltedly, and Jessica heard her own voice join in automatically.

When her shock began to wear off a little, it was replaced by a fiercely burning anger. This man had spent an entire morning in her house and had deliberately withheld his identity from her! To that calculated and underhanded deception he had added the insult of playing the despicable joke of masquerading as a handyman, helping her out of the goodness of his heart! No wonder he had looked at her as if he was secretly amused by something. She thought of the many times earlier that day when he could have told her who he was. Instead he had enjoyed himself at her expense.

She raged with resentment and humiliation, but she knew she had to master these emotions to save face. She would never let him see the effect his deception was having on her. She would not reveal how she really felt. No, she would never give him the satisfaction.

Keeping careful control of her voice, she managed to carry on a normal conversation. She saw with relief that

Iris and Carlotta were playing along beautifully. Their social instincts had taken over, instincts that dictated that they must remain unflappable. For the next few minutes small talk flowed quite smoothly. By the time Jessica and Peter Savage were ready to leave, Carlotta had recovered enough to fire a parting shot.

"How *very* neighborly it was of you, Mr. Wild—"

"Savage," Iris corrected, stifling a giggle.

"Oh, yes...to have troubled yourself this morning to come over to fix our plumbing—"

"Roof," Iris almost exploded.

Carlotta continued unperturbed. "If you need any help settling into *your* house, do let us know, won't you?"

Peter Savage appeared unmoved by her attempts at sarcasm. Ignoring the vitriolic emphasis on *"your* house," he smiled charmingly and said, "Thank you, that's most kind of you, Mrs. Romney. If I need any curtains run up or want to borrow a cup of sugar, I'll let you know."

Jessica hurried him out of the house before Carlotta had time to fully digest this pleasantry.

They walked in silence to his car, which Jessica saw with some annoyance was a Jeep, and a rather battered one at that. She hesitated for a moment on the passenger side. The step up was high, and her dress had a narrow skirt. But she had no alternative. She hitched her skirt up above her knees and, with a quick flash of long, slim legs, she was inside before he could help her.

She sat gingerly down on the cracked seat. He hopped in beside her and grinned. "Don't worry, I gave her a good going-over. She's as clean as a whistle."

"Oh, you shouldn't have fussed on my account," Jessica said sweetly, wriggling to find a comfortable spot on the lumpy seat.

"No trouble at all," he said generously. "I always give her a wash before I take a girl out in her."

Jessica turned away to hide a grimace.

"Just a sec," he said, lunging across her so suddenly that she pressed against the back of the seat in alarm.

Beyond Pride

"This seat belt is a little rusty and hard to do up unless you know the trick." He clicked the belt in place, leaning over her longer than was necessary. "There, it's done," he told her softly, looking straight into her eyes.

"Thank you," Jessica said faintly and looked away. Suddenly she was finding it difficult to fill her lungs with enough air.

For a while they drove in silence. Jessica's thoughts returned to nursing her resentment. Peter Savage was playing some sort of game with her, that much was obvious. But what, or why, she didn't know. Even coming to collect her in this decrepit Jeep had been a calculated provocation. From what little she had heard of the Romney estate's new owner, she knew him to be a very wealthy man. He must have a whole fleet of cars, yet he'd chosen this one for her. Perhaps, she thought caustically, it was the only one with a defective seat belt that he had to do up personally.

It seemed incredible that she was here beside him at all. She had met him only two days ago, and in that two days they had barely exchanged more than a dozen sentences. Yet in those two days they had become locked in some sort of contest of wills.

"I put in an order for the timber today," he said, breaking the silence. "I should be able to start work by the end of the week."

She turned to him, puzzled.

"On the bookshelves," he reminded her.

Jessica drew a deep breath. "Really, Mr. Savage, don't you think the joke's gone far enough?" she asked in a voice she barely managed to control.

"What joke is that?" he asked in surprise.

"Your clever little joke of being Mr. Handyman."

"But that's no joke." He stared at her. "I *am* a builder, as I told you when we first met."

And a whole lot you didn't tell me, Jessica thought. Aloud she said, "Is it a hobby of yours?"

"Hell, no. It's my living."

"It must be a very good one," she commented skeptically, thinking of the cost of buying the Romney estate.

"It is for me," he agreed. "I own my own company."

"Oh," she said and involuntarily glanced at his hands.

He caught her glance and held up one of his strong, work-hardened hands. "I don't use them so much these days except for paperwork, but if I never do another day's labor, they'll always stay this way," he said, and she thought she detected a note of pride and satisfaction in his voice.

She found that the hand held up for her inspection had the same effect on her that his gaze had had earlier, and she quickly looked away.

"But none of this can be much news to you," he continued. "You must have found out all this when I made the bid on your place." It was the first time he had referred to having bought Romney House.

"No. We didn't want to know much about who got our... who bought the house," she replied, hoping her voice betrayed no trace of bitterness. "Why? Did you make inquiries about us?"

He looked at her a moment before replying. "Not until I met you the other day."

A horrible idea occurred to her. "Is that why you came over to fix the roof for nothing, out of... charity?"

"No. I fixed the roof because I wanted to see you again. And I didn't do it for nothing. You're sitting beside me, aren't you? What's more, I'm going to build your bookshelves so I can ask you out again." He said it as matter-of-factly as if the whole thing were already settled.

Jessica swallowed a sharp retort and said instead, "I wonder how you ever became a wealthy man, Mr. Savage, with such unprofitable business dealings."

"If every client I had looked like you, I'd be a ruined man, Mrs. Romney," he said, grinning wickedly. "Is the weekend okay to begin work on the shelves?"

"No shelves, Mr. Savage. And this is our first and last date."

"Is it?" he asked, as if he knew better. "Then I'd

better make the most of it." Jessica shot him a quick glance, but his eyes were on the road ahead, his face expressionless.

Of course she should have expected it, Jessica told herself later, but even so she was quite unprepared for the place Peter Savage took her to for dinner. She looked about in disbelief as he brought the Jeep to a bumpy halt outside the town's shabbiest, most disreputable pub.

Sommerville, like every other Australian city, town, village, or two-shack settlement, had its fair share of watering holes, ranging from stately and historic hotels built in the last century to makeshift, corrugated-iron hovels. The Royal Victoria, despite its majestic name, was very much toward the bottom of the scale. Its customers were truckers, itinerant workers, and motorcycle gangs.

Only a couple of utility trucks stood in the dusty parking lot, along with half a dozen motorbikes leaning against a crumbling wall. As was the country tradition, the customers had come outside to drink their large schooners or middy glasses of strong draft beer, squatting on their heels against the walls, enjoying the cool evening.

Jessica's anger intensified. Was there to be no end to his crude and nasty surprises? Just what was he trying to prove?

As if to make an even bigger joke of their surroundings, Peter Savage leaped out of the car and hurried to her side to solicitously help her out. The drinkers gave an appreciative cheer at his gallantry.

When Jessica stepped down in full view of the men, the cheers increased and were supplemented with flattering comments. It was as if no one in living memory had ever seen the likes of Jessica Romney at the Royal Victoria.

She nodded at the men with just enough friendliness to avoid seeming haughty, which she sensed would be a fatal mistake, but with enough dignity to discourage further loud remarks. The men subsided into murmur and just before she stepped inside, she caught a look of admiration on Peter Savage's face.

She walked through the multicolored plastic strips that served as fly deterrent at the entrance and stopped inside the door. If such a thing were possible, the inside of the Royal Victoria was even tackier than the outside. She could see why the men preferred to drink outdoors.

The floor of the small, dark room was covered with cracked brown linoleum. The bar, of a faded red Formica, was pitted and scarred from a hundred deep cigarette burns, and the strip of toweling that stretched across it to catch the drip from glasses was as threadbare as a fishing net. Above the bar, over the dark, cracked mirror behind the shelves, hung fly-specked garlands of dusty gold and silver paper and Merry Christmas signs that might have been put up during the lifetime of the lady after whom the pub was named. There were several bar chairs, all with torn upholstery and foam rubber padding spilling out, and three rickety Formica tables, each surrounded by a motley collection of unsteady-looking chairs.

"Very nice," Jessica commented coolly. "But can we get in without a reservation?"

"I can," Savage told her, straight-faced. "I happen to know the owner."

"I'm impressed, Mr. Savage. And you only a newcomer in town." She stood for a moment undecided, as if she was having a hard time choosing a table. "That one over there, don't you think? It has such a good view of the whole room. We'll be able to see all the other guests arrive," she suggested.

"Well, if that isn't a coincidence." He shook his head in amazement. "That happens to be my regular table." He flashed her a smile, which she refused to return.

At that moment a still-handsome and virile man of about sixty came out of the back room. When he saw ter Savage, he hurried over to their table.

"day," he called in warm greeting. "How's it going,

Beyond Pride 31

"Fine, thanks, Charlie. Mrs. Romney, this is Charlie Travis, our host. He owns this four-star establishment. Charlie, I'd like you to meet Mrs. Romney."

"How do you do?" Jessica murmured politely, ignoring his astounded look when he recognized her name.

Charlie recovered quickly. "Good, love, real good. How's y'self?"

"Very thirsty," Jessica told him.

"Fix that in a jiffy, love. What'll you have?"

"Charlie has some passable wine, and he even knows how to mix a drink," Peter Savage volunteered.

"I'll have a beer, please," Jessica said.

"Coming right up," Charlie replied with approval. "Same for you, mate? Right, won't be a sec." He bustled off to the bar.

"I'd ask for a menu, but I don't think Charlie can write," Peter confided, leaning across the table.

Jessica raised her eyebrows. "They serve meals here?"

"My word, they do. And pretty tasty ones, too. Otherwise Charlie would lose the truckies' business. What would you like?"

"A meat pie, of course," Jessica said with resignation. Meat pies were to Australians what hot dogs were to Americans and fish-and-chips to the English. It was the main fare at most pubs, the first thing office workers, laborers, and schoolchildren grabbed for a quick lunch. They ranged in quality from tasteless masses of soggy pastry to succulent, rich-gravied delicacies in flaky homemade pastry. Jessica had come to like meat pies since she had settled in Australia, but she just hadn't expected them this evening.

Peter Savage laughed. "No, I think I'll splurge on you tonight. Nothing but the best." He threw her a glance to gauge her reaction, then went on. "Actually, Charlie makes the greatest Irish stew since my mother. He also has very decent steaks and a roast pork that will make you want to return again and again."

Jessica ignored the smirk on his face. "I'd like the very decent steak then, please. With some salad."

Charlie arrived with a small tray and handed her her beer with the greatest of care. "This one's on the house, love. Cheers." He took their order and, with another admiring glance at her and a wink at Savage, went off to cook their meal.

"Have you and Charlie been friends long?" Jessica asked.

"I met him on a trip here a couple of years ago."

"Oh. Then you knew Sommerville before... before you—"

"Yes. I've been here a few times. I often thought I would have liked to live here. You could say I was drawn to the place. Now I know why."

Jessica dropped her eyes to her glass. She rarely drank beer, especially since coming to Australia, where the brew was much more potent than in the States, but she felt the occasion called for it. She sipped daintily from her glass, feeling his eyes on her.

"You sip beer as if it were champagne," he remarked, having taken two large drafts of his own glass.

"I was taught never to gulp my food or drink."

"I'd like to hear everything you were taught..." he began, then stopped and let out a low laugh. Jessica followed his glance and saw that all the men who had been drinking outside had come in and were crowding around one end of the bar, trying to look as if they weren't staring at her.

"Do they bother you?" he asked.

"No, I can use all the diversion I can get," she told him pointedly.

She didn't find the men's attention displeasing, just a little disconcerting. It had been a long time since she had taken notice of such things. Her mouth relaxed into a smile.

"I didn't know you could do that!" Peter Savage marveled.

"What?" She frowned, then understood his meaning. She realized she must have seemed permanently sour to him, always in what Iris called a right royal huff. But was it any wonder? Ever since they'd met they'd been out of step with one another. Besides, a man who played such dirty tricks had no right to expect smiles.

Charlie brought their dinners, and Jessica realized Savage had been right. The food was good. The steak was juicy and thick, the salad fresh and crisp with a wonderful, unusual-tasting dressing. The plates and cutlery shone, and Jessica suspected they had been given an extra polish in her honor.

"Charlie was a cook in the navy for thirty years," Peter told her when she remarked on the excellent food.

"You know a lot about him."

"That much, anyway. See, I'm an ex-navy man myself."

"You were in the navy?" Jessica asked, interested despite herself. "Tell me about it."

He told her of his couple of years in the navy, which he had joined when he'd left school, then about his years as a builder's laborer, a miner, a stevedore, a station hand. He told her about the dozen other jobs he'd done in between. He spoke simply, without boasting, of the time he had spent working as hard as a coolie at various back-breaking jobs, of finally going back to laboring on building sites, of teaching himself engineering and drafting until he could draw up a plan as skillfully as any architect, of struggling to start his own construction company and finally building it into one of the most successful in the state.

Jessica listened with fascination to his tale of a truly self-made man. He had lost his parents when he was still in his teens and had had to leave school soon after. Everything there was to know about life he had taught himself. He was thirty-seven now and had no one in the world. He had been married once in his twenties, and though he didn't say much on that subject, Jessica sensed that it had been one of the more bitter experiences of his life. All he would say was that it hadn't stood the test of his early years of poverty.

In their first meetings he had seemed to Jessica a man

of few words. Now he spoke freely and fluently. As if reading her mind, he stopped abruptly.

"Now it's your turn. I'll give you equal time."

Jessica shook her head. "I haven't done half the things you have, not even a tenth, actually. There's not much to tell." But, by gently and skillfully drawing her out, he learned more about her than she had thought she was prepared to tell. She told him of her childhood in South Carolina, that she, too, had lost her parents when she was a teenager, though she had never experienced the hardships he had, because she had been taken in by wealthy relatives.

She told him of meeting her husband when he had been on a visit to the States, of coming to Australia as a bride, of settling in the new country and immediately loving it. Of Roderick's death she could not bring herself to speak, nor of the financial disaster that had followed.

But Peter seemed to understand. After looking at her for a while, he said, "It seems we're both against marrying again. You because you don't think you could ever repeat your experience, and me because I wouldn't want to repeat mine."

For an instant Jessica thought she saw the shadow of an old wound pass over his face. "Then..." She hesitated but went ahead with her question. "Then if you have no one and never want to, why did you buy an enormous place like Romney House?"

"Because from the first time I saw it, I wanted it. And when I want something, I take steps to get it." The tone of his voice, the way his eyes held hers, made the meaning behind his words unmistakable. He wasn't talking of the house alone.

Jessica's pulse raced. In an instant the easy rapport of the last half hour was over between them. "Then you'll have to learn, as I have had to, that you can't have everything you want, Mr. Savage," she said, her eyes pinpoints of green ice.

"That may be so, Mrs. Romney," he answered in a

voice of complete self-assurance, "but I'm a man who will die trying."

"I'd like to go now, please," Jessica said stiffly.

"Too much of a good thing?" he asked with a barely concealed smile.

"Far too much," she replied coldly. "And I think this game is just about played out, don't you? Your point, whatever that may be, must be made by now."

"My point?" he asked innocently.

"Bringing me here." She waved a hand around the sleazy bar. "In fact, taking me to dinner at all..."

"Oh, that," he said, no longer troubling to conceal the smile. "Well, that all started the other day when you called me 'young man.' No one has called me a young man in quite such a way since my third-class teacher tried to intimidate me. Now *there's* a woman I must take to dinner, I said to myself. And I knew just the place you'd love."

So that was it, Jessica thought. That was why he hadn't told her his name, why he had tricked her into accepting his invitation, why he had brought her here. The whole show had been directed toward putting her in her place.

Without another word she got up from the table and walked to the bar, where Charlie was washing glasses. She praised his cooking, thanked him, and, without counting it, took all the money from her purse and laid it on the bar.

"No, it's my treat," she insisted to the protesting Charlie. "I owed Mr. Savage. In fact, I feel I still owe him," she said half audibly as she headed outside.

By the time he caught up with her, she was already sitting in the Jeep, but try as she would she could not wrestle the seat belt into place.

Peter Savage leaned in on her side and, encircling her waist, reached to straighten the belt.

"An excellent law we have in this country, making the wearing of seat belts compulsory, don't you agree?

They ought to pass it in the States," he observed, looking into her eyes. For the first time in her life Jessica wondered how it would feel to sock someone in the jaw. She felt his strong arms about her waist, felt them as close as if there was no material between his skin and hers. She held her breath, afraid that if she let it out it would give her away, and sat staring straight ahead. It seemed an eternity before she heard the belt buckle click into place.

Peter Savage walked around to his own side, swung himself into the driver's seat, and turned to her. "Your place or mine?" he asked impudently and then laughed at the expression on her face. They drove home in almost complete silence.

He helped her from the Jeep and walked with her to the front door. "Since the evening was such a success, why don't we do it again tomorrow night?" he suggested brazenly.

"As I said earlier, Mr. Savage, this was our last date."

"Then, as I said earlier, I'd better make the most of it."

Without warning, his hands gripped her shoulders, and he pulled her to him. Then, in complete contrast to the rough, urgent movement, his lips descended on hers in a kiss so gentle and soft that it left her wondering if he had kissed her at all. Quickly he released her and stood back, looking down at her.

If the kiss had been more passionate or lingering, it could not have had the effect on her that this gentlest of touches did. The gesture, so unexpected from a man like him, touched not only her lips but her whole body.

Shaken, she took a step backward until she felt the support of the front door against her back. She waited until she could speak in a clear, icy voice.

"Someone should have told you, Mr. Savage, when you bought us out, that I do not come with the property." She turned and walked into the house.

chapter 4

"JESSICA, I WANT you to help me talk Mother into this dinner party, she's so set against it."

"Dinner party?" Jessica repeated vaguely, straightening her dressing table.

"You know, the one I mentioned yesterday," Iris explained. "For the Cuttlers. They're down from Sydney for the picnic races, and they're staying the whole week. It's been ages since we've seen them. Besides, I think it's high time we started entertaining again. We don't want people to think we're ashamed. I think we should fly in the face of poverty and show the world we don't give a damn!" she declared heroically.

"Yes, you're quite right," Jessica agreed, still a little preoccupied. "We ought to give a dinner for the Cuttlers."

Iris looked at her sister-in-law with curiosity. "Is something wrong, dear? You seem distracted this morning. Is something worrying you?"

"No, nothing at all," Jessica said hastily with a bright smile. "I have a few business matters on my mind, that's all."

"Are you sure?" Iris insisted, adding with a sly smile, "Sure it wasn't something that happened last night with that yummy man?"

Jessica made a grimace of exasperation at her sister-in-law. She wasn't going to let her start that again. Iris had waited up for her the night before and had continued her third degree as soon as she had awakened this morning.

Jessica had told her as little as possible, just that they had gone to dinner at a "little out of the way place," had come home, said good night, and that had been that. But Iris, who seemed absolutely fascinated with Peter Savage, would not leave the subject alone.

"Well, I think the whole thing is just too romantic. Not telling you who he was and coming to do odd jobs around the house. He must have been smitten with you from the first time you met on the road." She sighed dramatically.

Jessica made an inelegant sound. "Take my word for it, Iris, the man's motives were very far from romantic."

"All I can say," Iris insisted, "is that he turned out to be a most pleasant surprise. I almost don't mind losing Romney House if it means living next door to him." At Jessica's reproachful look, she added hastily, "Well of course I do mind, you know that, but all I can say is—"

"Yes, it seems it is all you can say," Jessica interrupted impatiently. "You've been saying it all morning."

"But sweetie, it can't be said often enough. The man is a gift from heaven. Divinely attractive. I just adore that rugged, sunburned look. And those piercing blue eyes... Rich, and right next door."

"I don't think he's a gift meant for us," Jessica said.

"Jessica, I hope you didn't say anything to turn the man away," Iris cried in alarm. "I know how frosty you can get when you mean to discourage someone. Did you?"

"Just don't expect him to come knocking on our door for a cup of sugar," Jessica said.

"You mean you did discourage him?" Iris wailed.

"I didn't have to. We both realized at once that ours wasn't meant to be an enduring friendship," she replied dryly.

"Oh, Jessie, but the man is sooo divine—"

Jessica cut her off firmly. "About the dinner, Iris dear.

I think it's a very good idea. Why don't you work out a menu right now? Don't worry about Carlotta. I'll work on her."

"You might have a hard time," Iris warned. "She's still reeling from the shock of last night. The poor dear is rather confused about the whole thing. Can't understand why a millionaire goes around disguising himself, fixing people's plumbing."

"Oh dear," Jessica said, and the two collapsed in helpless laughter. When they recovered, Iris went happily away to the task she most enjoyed doing, determined to plan a meal that would prove to the world that, though the Romneys might have slipped a little, they still knew how to entertain on a grand scale.

Jessica sank wearily into the little chintz-covered chaise in the window recess of her room. She had had a restless night, full of disjointed, crazy dreams about Peter Savage. She was annoyed with herself for letting him intrude into her dreams and now into most of her waking thoughts as well. No matter what she had attempted to do that morning, no matter how she tried to immerse herself in work, she could only command half her mind to pay attention. The other half kept wandering independently back to the subject of Peter Savage.

And the man certainly wasn't worth another moment's thought. The insufferable, arrogant, insolent, self-assured... He had actually looked her straight in the eye and as much as told her that he wanted to... Jessica directed a hateful glance toward Romney House, the roof of which was just visible from her bedroom window.

Never, never in her life had she been treated like that. She was used to having men admire her, but it was a respectful, distant admiration, not this crude approach. When she thought of the gentle, almost reverent way Roderick had courted her... But she wouldn't think of Roderick now. She wouldn't put him in the same thought process as this man.

In her more honest moments Jessica had to admit that she did deserve at least some of the treatment. She *had* acted condescending. But surely she did not deserve such insolence from him. To confuse her further, there had been his kiss. Her hand flew to her mouth at the memory. His kiss had been so gently sweet, providing such a contradictory ending to the evening. For a long time she sat on the chaise, staring blindly into space, before she roused herself. "Fool," she muttered, "sitting here mooning like a teenager when there are so many important things that need your attention." She forced her mind to the dinner party she had discussed with Iris.

Mr. and Mrs. Cuttler had been friends of Carlotta and her late husband for many years. Eric, their only child, had gone to school with Roderick, and the two had remained friends until Roderick's death. The Cuttlers were extremely wealthy and had great social aspirations. They lived most of the time in Sydney and, like many of the well-heeled people of Sommerville and its surrounding area, were "Pitt Street farmers"—Pitt Street was Sydney's Wall Street—who spent only weekends and holidays on their property. In the friendship between the Romneys and the Cuttlers there had always been an element of rivalry in which, until now, Carlotta had had the upper hand. She considered her family, whose wealth and prominence could be traced back to the early days of Australia's colonization, superior to that of the Cuttlers, who had been moneyed for only two generations.

Such things had mattered in Carlotta's world, and Jessica knew it would not be easy for her mother-in-law to face these people in her new circumstances. But it was time Carlotta was eased into the realities of her new life.

At thirty-five Eric Cuttler was still a bachelor, committed to running the many Cuttler enterprises that had been handed over to him by his now retired father. One of the great differences between Eric and Roderick had always been that Eric had loved making money while Roderick had never had a desire to. So as the Romney fortunes had dwindled, the Cuttlers' had multiplied.

Jessica knew that Eric had always been a little in love with her. From the moment Roderick had introduced them, Eric had been smitten, but since he kept his feelings to a frank and distant devotion, Jessica shrugged it off, as only a woman who is used to admirers even after marriage can.

Eric had often been on hand to help untangle the financial mess after her husband's death, and he continued to be a solicitous friend. But Jessica had a feeling that she had only to ask and he would be happy to be anything more she wished.

Of course she had never had the slightest inclination, but now... Suddenly an idea, a very satisfying idea, began to take shape. She paced the floor in her room. Yes, it would be perfect!

Half an hour later she knocked on Iris's door. "It took a bit of doing, but I've won Carlotta over to the idea of the dinner," she announced.

"Oh, lovely! How did you do it?"

"Stirred a few snobbish feelings in her. Told her it was her duty as a Romney to keep up a good front. Told her that if she didn't, Gwen Cuttler and all her other friends would start to feel sorry for her."

"That must have done it!" Iris exclaimed with admiration.

"It did it, all right. By the time I left, she was considering the guest list."

"A guest list? Then we'll have more than just the Cuttlers?"

"Might as well, since we're going to all the trouble. Do you think you could manage the cooking if we got Mrs. Green in to help in the kitchen that night?"

"Like a breeze. I'll be magnificent," Iris promised grandly.

"Then what do you say to ten people?"

"Perfect. Who are they?"

"The three of us, the three Cuttlers—that's six, the Phillipses—that's eight, Marjorie Cunningham—that's nine, and Mr. Savage." This last Jessica added so nonchalantly that it was a few seconds before the name struck Iris.

"Did I hear you right?" she asked in disbelief.

"You did," Jessica replied calmly.

"But wait a minute," Iris protested, her eyes widening with excitement, "only a half hour ago you were saying—"

"I've reconsidered," Jessica replied coolly. "I think it would be neighborly to invite Mr. Savage."

Iris looked at her suspiciously. "But why did you change your mind?"

"Just a couple of unimportant reasons." Jessica shrugged evasively.

"Oh, goody," Iris exclaimed with glee. "I sense intrigue."

"Only because you're far too nosy," Jessica threw over her shoulder as she left the room.

Back in her own room she went to the window and looked across at Romney House. For a moment she had a small panicky doubt, but it dissolved quickly. This should take care of Mr. Savage. He had tried to put her in her place; she would put him in his. He had taken her to the sleaziest place in town for a perverse joke of his own; she would invite him to dinner with the greatest snobs in town and see how comfortable he would feel.

And then there would be Eric, who, at the slightest encouragement, would stick to her side like glue. Mr. Savage could not help but get the picture. All in all, it promised to be a very purposeful dinner party.

The dining room was situated at the back of the house. On this mild October evening the French doors leading onto the shaded, black and white marble-flagged veranda were wide open. Beyond the veranda stretched the back garden, from which a light breeze carried in the fragrance of jasmine and the ceaseless vibrating chorus of cicadas.

The oval dining table, extended tonight to seat ten, was already set. The heavy cream-colored Irish linen tablecloth and its matching lace-edged, monogrammed napkins were crisp with starch. Weighty Victorian silver shone next to Royal Doulton china edged in gold and burgundy. Before each setting stood four crystal goblets—for water, white wine, claret, and champagne. Iris's plans for tonight had been extravagant. In the center of the table stood two enormous crystal and bronze candelabra, their tall cream-colored wax candles waiting to be lit. Also at the center, among silver-and-crystal cruets and saltcellars, stood small silver bowls of red and cream-colored roses.

Jessica looked around the dining room with its warm, peach-colored walls, its brown, cream-veined marble fireplace, cream woodwork, clusters of miniatures, crystal sconces, fruitwood furniture, and needlepoint rugs. To other people it must be difficult to imagine that it was the home of three women who had "come down" in the world, she realized. Only those who had known the Romneys when thirty people had sat down to dinner in a room five times the size of this, who knew that there had once been eight candelabra instead of two and that the silver was only second best because the more valuable Georgian service had had to be sold, and who remembered that once maids had served at their table—only they would realize how much things had changed.

With everything ready for the arrival of the guests, Jessica went up to her room to prepare for the evening. All afternoon Carlotta had been acting like a martyr about to go to the stake. Iris, who loved parties and knew her meal had turned out superbly, had been filled with excitement. But Jessica felt nervous determination. For the first time in her life she experienced the jitters that normally beset less self-confident hostesses.

The cause of her nervousness wasn't that the Cuttlers, Phillipses, and Marjorie Cunningham would be seeing them in their new home for the first time. Jessica hadn't given a single thought to that. It was the invitation to Peter Savage, which she had begun to regret almost the minute she'd sent it. He had accepted promptly and formally, and there was nothing she could do about it now. But what had seemed like a good idea a few days before now seemed like a terrible mistake.

When she had decided to include him in the party, she had still been in the grip of anger and resentment. She'd longed to pay him back some way. Now, after almost a week, she felt differently. She wanted only never to see him again. That, of course, would be impossible in the long run, since he was now their neighbor. And while he had made no attempt to contact her since their date, she knew it was inevitable that in such a small community she would run into him sooner or later. Maybe, she consoled herself, it was best this way. The party should draw the line between them for once and for all.

Jessica agonized over the possibility that he might have regarded her invitation as a sign that she had enjoyed her evening with him and wanted to see him again. God forbid! But the presence of Eric and the attention she would lavish on him should take care of that. As for how Eric would take it—she'd just have to face one problem at a time.

Jessica put on a soft green chiffon dress that was the exact color of her eyes. Made especially for her by one of Sydney's top designers, it fit her so perfectly that she looked like a slender, floating vision in it. The top was a simple halter style that flattered her smooth, lightly tanned arms and shoulders. The skirt flared in gentle folds from a narrow waist and fell just the correct distance from her silver sandals.

Jessica brushed her honey-brown hair into a simple style, parted in the middle with soft waves to her shoulders. Two small flat discs of pavé diamonds in her ears were her only adornment. Then a minimum of makeup— peach-colored blusher and a hint of eyeshadow, not enough to detract from her large, black-fringed green eyes. A peach-pink lipstick, a dash of perfume, and she stood back to eye the result. It would do. She had learned long ago that the less she fussed, the more finished-looking the result.

On her way downstairs she stopped and knocked on Iris' door. Iris did not subscribe to Jessica's philosophy of "less is best." She delighted in fussing in front of her mirror for hours. When Jessica came in, she was sitting at her dressing table with piles of discarded makeup and jewelry in front of her. She turned to look Jessica over.

"Perfect as always. Like a magazine cover. Now be a darling and help me decide. I've tried on practically everything I own, and I still don't know."

"You must have." Jessica grimaced as she looked around the room, in which clothes of all colors and styles were strewn haphazardly about. Her sister-in-law's taste leaned toward the spectacular. Jessica knew better than to advise her to wear something simple. There was no such thing in her wardrobe. But with her dramatic red hair, creamy white skin, and sapphire eyes, her outlandish clothes looked good on her.

"That one," Jessica said after pretending to ponder the selection. She pointed to a gown heavily embroidered in purple and silver beads.

"I was thinking of that one myself," Iris said happily, but a frown of doubt appeared on her face. "But do you think—"

"You'll look divine in it," Jessica hastened to assure her, using Iris' favorite adjective to clinch the matter. "Now don't be too long. They should be arriving any minute," she called over her shoulder.

Next she went to Carlotta's room. Even before she opened the door she could smell the heavy scent of gardenia, a perfume Carlotta always wore. Mrs. Green was just helping her into her dress.

"Don't she look good?" Mrs. Green demanded proudly, looking at Carlotta with admiration. Mrs. Green, gray-haired and plump, was fascinated by all the Romney women, especially by Carlotta, who was about her own age and who looked as different from her as a pampered woman can from a work-worn one.

"She does, indeed," Jessica said, fussing over her mother-in-law.

Carlotta looked regal in a high-necked, midnight-blue gown with wide, floating sleeves. She gave a deep sigh and said in a tearful voice, "If only I still had my sapphires. I had this dress made to match them, you know."

Jessica remembered the especially cruel blow of having had to sell most of their important pieces of jewelry.

"Sapphires would be gilding the lily anyway," she told Carlotta cheerfully.

"Of course they would, love," Mrs. Green agreed. "You don't want no fancy jewelry to make you look nicer. Why, any woman twenty years younger would give anything to look like you tonight."

Jessica silently blessed Mrs. Green.

"Ah, well..." Carlotta let out a less forlorn sigh. "Mrs. Green, perhaps you had better go downstairs now. Our guests will be arriving shortly, and you should be on hand to open the door."

"I'll take care of the door," Jessica said. "Mrs. Green is needed in the kitchen."

"Do you think you should?" Carlotta asked, worried.

"What, open the door myself?" Jessica laughed. "Of course I should. The best of families are doing it now, you know." As she went down the stairs, she wondered with an inward sigh how long it would take Carlotta to adjust to the way things were.

The doorbell rang almost the moment she reached the hall. She felt an instant of panic and was immediately furious with herself. But it was only the Phillipses.

Colonel and Mrs. Phillips, like the Romneys, were year-round residents of Sommerville. They had a small house in Palm Beach, the luxurious seaside community north of Sydney, but they spent most of their time here on their property, where Mr. Phillips bred horses and Mrs. Phillips was a member of every horsey club going, from the local pony club to the ladies' racing committee. They were a middle-aged couple, lifetime acquaintances of the Romneys, and, apart from horses, they had few interests in life.

Colonel Phillips was a jovial giant of a man in a well-worn dinner suit that must have seen at least twenty years' service. His wife was likewise shabbily dressed

Beyond Pride

in a gown she had worn to every dinner party for the last three years. It was common knowledge that the Phillipses would rather spend money on horse blankets than on frivolities like clothes.

Jessica led them into the drawing room and poured them drinks, and soon they were joined by Iris and Carlotta. A few minutes later the bell rang again and the three Cuttlers and Marjorie Cunningham arrived at almost the same time.

Marjorie was a woman in her forties who lived alone and ran the farm her parents had left her. Waratah, her property, was second in size only to the Romney estate, and her distinction in life was that her family had been the very first white settlers in the region. There were rumors of convicts in her ancestry—the first settlers who were transported from England's jails two hundred years before to found a penal colony, a distinction that Australians claimed with pride.

Marjorie Cunningham spoke with a clipped English accent, though she had never set foot in England and was considered by the locals, with an almost proprietary pride, to be the greatest snob in the district.

The Cuttlers were a plump, expensively dressed couple who believed themselves very wordly because they spent almost half of the year abroad and could drop names on three continents. Eric, a tall, dark, good-looking man, appeared very dapper tonight in his well-tailored dinner clothes. Jessica liked him and was grateful to him for his help, but she couldn't help being a little bored by his self-satisfaction. He regarded her warmly, and his hand lingered in hers when they greeted each other. It would be easy to create the impression that they were devoted to each other.

The rivalry between Carlotta and Gwen Cuttler had always been keen, and tonight Mrs. Cuttler began by making the mistake of trying to turn the situation to her advantage. When she entered the drawing room, she approached Carlotta with outstretched arms and a sympathetic look on her face. She murmured something about what a shame it all was... how shockingly cruel... and if there was anything, *anything at all* she could do to help...

Her words produced the exact result Jessica had hoped for. Carlotta grew inches taller, her eyes took on a steely glint, and thereafter she majestically repulsed every one of Gwen Cuttler's attempts to be patronizing.

When the doorbell rang once again, Jessica's earlier panic returned. This time there could be no doubt who it was. Jessica signaled to Iris.

"Would you mind getting the door? I'm just about to refill Marjorie's glass," she lied.

"Delighted!" Iris exclaimed and made her best stage exit toward the door.

Jessica made sure her back was turned when he entered the room. She didn't turn around again until Iris was already making the introductions.

It had been almost a week since Jessica had seen him; in that time his face had been in her thoughts many times. But nothing had prepared her for the impact of his presence. She felt as if everyone and everything had faded into the background. His hair shone with an electric, golden light, and as he shook hands with the other guests, he looked as if a black tie and dinner jacket had been invented especially for him.

She saw the amazement and curiosity with which the other guests turned to him. Peter Savage's entrance had been a complete surprise to them. They had not expected that the Romneys, who had a good reason to avoid him, would have included him in tonight's dinner party. Jessica caught snatches of their whispered speculations and sensed their anticipation. The prospect of spending an evening with this mystery man clearly delighted them.

When Peter Savage had finally been introduced to everyone else, his eyes sought out and found Jessica. He gave her a slow smile of recognition and came over to where she was standing.

Standing so that she was shielded from the rest of the company, he took her hand. "Mrs. Romney, how kind of you to invite me," he said formally, his eyes searching hers intently.

"Very pleased you could come, Mr. Savage," she replied with equal formality.

"I'm pleased you're pleased. Especially since a few days ago I thought the door of your house had been slammed in my face forever. What made you change your mind?"

Jessica, who had hoped he'd have the tact not to bring that subject up, narrowed her eyes. "It's a little custom we have around these parts, Mr. Savage. It's called good manners. Welcoming a new neighbor is part of it."

"I see," he said, obviously unconvinced. "You must teach me about these quaint customs someday. I find them a bit confusing. First you tell a man you never want to see him again, then you give a party to welcome him. A little out of sequence, isn't it?"

"You're making one mistake, Mr. Savage. The party's not for you. It's... it's for Eric Cuttler," Jessica improvised.

"Him?" He jerked his head questioningly in Eric's direction.

Jessica nodded.

"Hmm," he said, taking the other man's measure. "He doesn't look like a bloke who gets doors slammed in his face."

"He isn't," she assured him.

"Are you speaking from personal experience, or did his mother tell you that?" he asked with a cheeky grin. As she made a move to walk away, he put a detaining hand on her arm. "Anyway, I'm glad you have such good manners and invited me. It solved a great personal problem for me."

"What problem?" Jessica asked, curious in spite of herself.

"The problem of how I was going to get to see you again." He was talking in a way that isolated them from the rest of the room. Jessica became conscious of her guests' curious glances and used the attention they were drawing as an excuse to draw away. She would *not* be cornered by him again that evening.

When they went in to dinner, she pointedly took Eric's arm. Delighted with this attention, he rarely left her side for the rest of the evening. He was seated next to her at dinner, while Peter Savage sat directly opposite. Jessica wished she had not left the seating arrangements to Iris. But at least Peter was wedged in between Marjorie and Mrs. Cuttler, both relentless chatterers and probers into other people's business. They would keep him captive through dinner, Jessica surmised.

The soup was not yet removed before Marjorie began. "What made you decide to settle in our part of the world, Mr. Savage? Most of our people are *old* families. We get very few newcomers," she commented in her affected accent.

"I've liked the place ever since I worked as a kid in the sandstone quarry outside of town," Peter Savage told her, calmly eating his soup while all eyes became riveted on him.

"Worked as...you mean..." Marjorie began, looking at him incredulously.

He finished his soup, put down his spoon, wiped his mouth on his napkin, and turned to her. "Yes, I spent a summer laboring in the quarries here, which I see with regret are closed now. I've always been interested in colonial architecture, especially in sandstone buildings, so I thought working in a quarry for a while would be a good education. I spent my free time walking about town looking at the buildings. You know, I've been all over Australia, but I haven't found Sommerville's equal yet in fine sandstone architecture."

"Well, of course," Marjorie said, bristling with pride. "Most of our buildings are under the protection of the National Trust now, you know. We've been declared a historic area. When my family first settled here back in—"

But Gwen Cuttler interrupted. "You mean you're an architect, Mr. Savage?" she asked.

Beyond Pride

"No, a builder," he replied and went on to explain the difference between an architect, who had a formal education, and a man like himself, who had acquired the same skills through long, hard hours of work.

The guests fell silent as they digested this piece of information. Marjorie raised an eyebrow at Gwen Cuttler, which made Jessica want to give her a swift kick under the table. She could not help admiring the straightforward, unselfconscious manner in which Peter Savage had explained himself. He was neither defiant nor defensive nor apologetic. He was simply matter-of-fact.

Just then Eric cleared his throat in a way that Jessica knew meant he was about to say something pompous. "I don't wonder you admire our local architecture, Mr. Savage," he began. "There's certainly nothing to recommend the houses you builders are putting up these days."

"Only that they shelter people, Mr. Cuttler," he replied.

"But must it be done in such a graceless, unimaginative manner?" Eric persisted.

"It must for most people who don't have the money to indulge their imaginations."

"Personally, I'd prefer to live in a tent rather than in one of your squalid modern structures," Eric declared.

"If you lived on the basic wage, you'd probably have to," Savage remarked, shooting him an ironic look.

"Perhaps if building contractors were more honest and not always out to make a quick buck, people would get a better deal on their houses," Eric persisted.

This was such an obvious dig at Savage and the way he had made his fortune that Jessica held her breath as they all waited for his reaction.

But Peter Savage remained unmoved by the insult. Giving the other man a scornful glance, he said evenly, "If we were *all* more honest and *none* of us was out to make a quick buck, all things would be equal. Then we'd all live in exactly the same sort of house—probably one of those squalid modern structures."

Well, Jessica thought, it was obvious that Eric Cuttler and Peter Savage would not be the greatest of friends. She just wished Eric hadn't made quite such an ass of himself.

For a while the conversation drifted to other topics, but Gwen and Marjorie, both obviously burning with curiosity about the newcomer, soon brought the topic back to him.

"Tell me, Mr. Savage, do you mean to stay in Sommerville most of the time, or will your business keep you away?" Gwen began.

Savage turned from her and looked straight at Jessica as he answered, "At the moment nothing could keep me away from here."

All eyes shifted instantly to Jessica. Eric began to clear his throat, but Savage had already turned back to Gwen. "I want to settle into your wonderful town as quickly as I can. I have a lot to do, so I'll be around for a while."

Though his glance at her had been brief and his answer could have meant anything, Jessica felt as if he had made a loud announcement to everyone in the room. She immediately began a very animated conversation with Eric.

"Do you ride, Mr. Savage?" Colonel Phillips asked the question nearest to his heart.

"Years ago I worked as a stockman on a cattle station up in Queensland. To that extent I can stay on a horse," Savage replied.

"Oh," Mrs. Phillips responded with raised eyebrows. Jessica stifled a smile. She knew the kind of grueling horsemanship it took to be a stockman—the Australian version of a cowboy—in the merciless heat and vast emptiness of the cattle stations of the north, so very different from the genteel English style of riding of which the Phillipses were devotees.

When the subject of riding was exhausted, Gwen Cuttler brought up her favorite topic. "You really must take time off, Mr. Savage, and do some traveling abroad. I can give you some very good addresses. We have met so many important people on the Continent."

Savage informed her that he had already traveled extensively, and while he admired Europe, the wilds of South America and Asia were really more his cup of tea.

Inevitably Marjorie brought up the subject of families, questioning him about his in a not-too-subtle manner and going extensively into her own pedigree.

"That's very interesting," Savage remarked after listening to her for some time. "I myself had an uncle who spent a great part of his life in jail."

Iris let out a shriek of laughter, and for the moment Marjorie was effectively quelled.

It seemed Peter Savage was determined to deprive the company of the pleasure of patronizing him on any subject, Jessica thought with amusement. If she had meant to discomfit him by throwing him into the ring with the Sommerville establishment, she had not succeeded. But then, neither had he managed to put a dent in her composure when he had subjected her to the same sort of thing, she thought with satisfaction. The score remained even.

The dinner was a great success. Course after course brought enthusiastic exclamations. The fresh green-pea soup, the seafood terrine, the quail, the crisply steamed, buttered, garden-grown vegetables, the light, creamy raspberry soufflé—all were excellent. Iris basked in the glow of achievement, and even Carlotta seemed to forget for the moment that there was no cook in the kitchen or help at the table.

Jessica and Peter Savage exchanged few words during dinner, but several times he suddenly turned to her in the middle of a sentence, making her feel as if they were alone in the room. It was as if he were making love to her across the table, as if she were being touched by him. At such times she would turn, flushed, to Eric and make vivacious conversation. But soon, as if by a magnet, her attention would be drawn back across the table.

When they rose at last to take coffee and liqueur in the drawing room, Jessica attached herself to Eric's arm and made sure they took their seats as far as possible from where Peter Savage sat.

It was not the least bit difficult to engage Eric's exclusive attention, and soon she found herself listening, a little impatiently, to a detailed account of a great business coup he had made in Sydney. So much for chasing a quick buck, she thought with irony. She tried hard to concentrate but could not give him her full attention. Savage's presence in the room made that impossible. She could neither see nor hear him, yet he was the only person she was fully aware of.

She had to get away to be quietly by herself for a while. Pleading some household matter that needed her attention, she hurried from the room. In the hall she paused for a moment before heading for the kitchen.

Mrs. Green was elbow deep in suds and dinner dishes.

"I've come to give you a hand," Jessica said, reaching for a towel.

"No, love, you can't do that!" Mrs. Green protested. "You shouldn't even be in here. You'll get that pretty frock dirty."

"I'll put an apron on," she said and tied one of Mrs. Green's around her waist.

"But there's no need for that, love. I can manage on me own."

"I'm going to help you, Mrs. Green; otherwise you'll never get through this pile of stuff."

"What, me?" Mrs. Green gave a snort. "I get through this much and more every night. I got nine at home."

"Children?" Jessica cried.

"Yeah, nine kids. An' all of 'em living with me and Dad still," she said proudly.

A small, familiar ache shot through Jessica at the mention of children. If only she and Roderick...

"They reckon they can't get cookin' like Mum's anywhere else," Mrs. Green said with a laugh. "Still, I suppose they'll be leavin' one day or another to get married and such. Here, love, leave them big dishes for me. Just wipe them plates if you're so set on helpin', though

Beyond Pride

I don't know what you want to for."

Despite her protest, Mrs. Green seemed very pleased to have company. She chatted on happily, her busy, work-reddened hands not stopping for a moment. Jessica was grateful for the distraction.

She was wiping the silverware and Mrs. Green was describing her seventh child when the door opened and Peter Savage's head appeared. Jessica's pulse raced, and she turned toward the sink in dismay. So much for her clever escape!

"Need a hand?" he offered.

Mrs. Green chuckled. "Now what would I do with a fancy-dressed bloke like you in me kitchen? You two young ones shouldn't be wastin' your time here. Run along now and enjoy yourselves."

Savage took his jacket off and hung it on the back of a kitchen chair. "I always like to earn my supper," he said with an elaborate wink at Mrs. Green, who responded with another snort of laughter. He reached for a clean cloth and a wet plate.

"Really, Mr. Savage, there's no need for that," Jessica protested stiffly.

"Really, Mrs. Romney, I want to." He reached for another plate.

Jessica turned to the other woman. "Mrs. Green, this is Mr. Savage, expert quarry worker, expert builder, expert horseman, expert business tycoon, expert world traveler, and, no doubt he'll tell you, expert dish wiper."

"As a matter of fact, I did work as a busboy once at a summer resort on the Barrier Reef," he said, straight-faced.

"Well then, you should know enough to roll them sleeves up before they get dirty," Mrs. Green said, eyeing his dazzling white dress shirt.

"Would you?" he asked, holding his two arms out to Jessica, both his hands being occupied. She had no choice but to remove the dark sapphire cuff links and roll the crisp white sleeves up to just below the elbow. She couldn't help noticing that his muscular forearms were tanned a reddish-brown, the hairs glistening like gold under the kitchen light. Jessica's hands brushed against his skin. She felt his eyes on her, but didn't look up. She had come to the kitchen to get away from him, and here she was so close that she could hear his breathing and see the rise and fall of his chest.

"Thank you," he said, still not taking his eyes off her. "Now, if you'll just get one of those towels and tie it around my waist..."

"I thought you came to the kitchen to help!" Jessica flared.

"I came to find you." His eyes traveled slowly over her. "You look very lovely tonight, but you shouldn't have dressed up on my account. I like you best with bare legs and dirty knees." Remembering the morning he had caught her working in the garden, Jessica flushed and changed the subject quickly.

"Mrs. Green has been telling me that she has nine children."

Savage whistled in admiration. "That's an achievement to be proud of, all right, Mrs. Green."

The older woman looked extremely pleased. "That's what you need up at that big house you've bought," she said. "You should fill the place up with kids."

Peter Savage's face lit up. "I *knew* I had to fill it with something! I was thinking more along the lines of furniture, but I think yours is a much better idea. What do you think?" He turned to Jessica.

"Having heard you on the subject of marriage, I think you had better stick with furniture," she replied.

He was about to respond when the door opened again, and Eric peered in. Jessica made a great show of welcoming him.

"Yes, come on in, there's plenty for everyone," Savage invited, throwing him a towel.

Eric caught it awkwardly and looked at it as if it were a foreign object. But he refused to be left out. Gingerly he picked up a plate and immediately dropped it. The plate smashed into pieces.

Beyond Pride 57

"Strewth!" Mrs. Green muttered under her breath.

Savage tut-tutted and shook his head in an infuriating manner. Jessica glared at him as she stooped down beside Eric to pick up the pieces.

"What's going on in here?" Iris's voice called gaily from the door. She stood surveying the scene. "Have I missed anything? Were you hurling plates at each other?" she asked eagerly. "Jessica, trust you to carry off the only two attractive men in the room. Where were you boys, I'd like to know, when I was slaving over a hot stove all day?"

Mrs. Green poured coffee into kitchen cups, and Iris got out some sherry and they had an impromptu party in the kitchen.

"Marjorie and the Phillipses were just talking about the Lilac Ball," Iris said, sipping her sherry-laced coffee. "You haven't lived until you've been to our Lilac Ball, Mr. Savage. It's the gayest thing going since Queen Victoria's funeral, but if you manage to sneak enough drinkies under the noses of the old fogies who're on the committee, and if you like to dance, it can turn into quite a scream. Will you come?"

"It sounds like something I can't afford to miss," he said.

"Oh, good!" Iris cried, jumping off the edge of the kitchen table. "Let's make a little party of our own and scandalize everyone by enjoying ourselves."

"I don't think we should go quite that far to break with tradition," Jessica remarked dryly. The Lilac Ball was quite the most boring event of all the Sommerville social obligations. "I think I'll join the others now. Carlotta must be wondering where we've gotten to," she added.

She spent the rest of the evening by Eric's side, avoiding Peter Savage. But when the guests were leaving, she had to face him again.

"I enjoyed tonight very much," he told her, adding in an amused undertone, "though I'm not so sure I was meant to."

Jessica gave him a quick look and realized a little shamefacedly that he had guessed at least part of her reason for inviting him.

"Would you let me take you to the ball?" he asked.

"I'm sorry, but Eric has already asked me," she lied, praying silently that Eric would still be in town that night to bear out her lie.

She had the satisfaction of seeing a look of displeasure cross Peter Savage's face.

chapter 5

THE NEXT MORNING Jessica was in the study working on some accounts when the doorbell rang. She went to answer the door.

"Eric!" She regarded her visitor with surprise. "What brings you here so early?"

"I hope I'm not intruding," he apologized.

Guiltily she realized that she hadn't given him a single thought since last night. Considering the rather misleading attention she had lavished on him the night before, he was entitled to a more friendly welcome.

"Of course not, very pleased to see you," she said, putting more warmth into her voice. "I was just going over some papers in the study. Why don't we sit in there?"

"That's one of the reasons I'm calling," Eric said, following her. "I want to offer my help with any business problems you might have."

"You're really very kind," Jessica said gratefully, "but I think I have everything pretty well under control now. You really were the greatest help after Roderick died. I don't know what we would have done without your advice."

"It can't be easy for you, I know," he said with sympathy.

"Oh, but it's not so bad," she protested cheerfully. "We've settled in here now, and we have enough income to get by, thanks to your sound advice about renting those properties. The debts have all been paid and there's no mortgage hanging over us, so we're really better off than most people."

"I really admire you—everyone does—for the way you've managed things and kept the family together," Eric said earnestly. He shook his head. "But all this responsibility on your shoulders. I know Iris and Carlotta can't be much help."

"Do you know, I've quite come to enjoy the responsibilities," Jessica told him. "I've found a great deal of satisfaction in juggling and balancing and having it all come out right in the end. I think even Iris is enjoying herself. She's become a genius in the kitchen."

"You don't have to convince me of that after last night," Eric said, patting his stomach. "What about Carlotta?"

"Oh, well." Jessica shrugged. "It's much harder for her than for us."

"She certainly seemed in fine form last night. Keeping my mother in her place put her in fine spirits."

"You know Carlotta." Jessica laughed. "She always rises to the occasion." She could see that there was something else on Eric's mind. Finally he came out with it.

"That chap Savage—rather full of himself, isn't he? Doesn't make a nuisance of himself around here, does he?" he asked uneasily.

"No...no," Jessica replied, averting her eyes. "We've really only met him a couple of times, and after last night I feel our social obligations toward him are just about discharged. I...we don't expect to see much of him at all." She found it hard not to smile at the obvious relief on Eric's face. So *that* was the reason for his early call. He wanted to find out how Savage stood with the Romneys, or rather, she suspected, with herself.

She studied Eric closely and wondered why she wasn't attracted to him. He was good-looking, well educated, well traveled, sophisticated, wealthy, and had an authoritative manner many women found irresistible—though he was just a trifle too conscious of the schools he had attended, the clubs he belonged to, the positions he held. How little any of those things had meant to Roderick.

"It's a shame Romney House had to go to a chap like that," Eric said now.

"I don't know." Jessica shrugged again. "At least he has no plans to turn it into a motel."

"Well, I doubt he'll ever fit in with our crowd."

"I doubt he wants to," she replied.

"Good morning, Eric darling," Iris trilled from the doorway. "Haven't come to complain to me of food poisoning, have you?"

The two had been playmates since childhood, and Eric's stuffy manner always wilted under Iris's familiar and good-humored badinage.

"Expect to hear from my lawyers on that by tomorrow," he kidded back. "No, I'm here to ask Jessica if I can take her to the Lilac Ball."

Having already planned to go with him, Jessica accepted promptly. When she returned from seeing him to the door, Iris looked at her thoughtfully.

"Jessie, you're not keen on Eric, are you?" she asked in her abrupt way.

"Not a bit," Jessica admitted.

"I thought not," Iris said. "You know, I've been thinking that *there* is a perfectly good man going to waste. When I think of all that money and the things I could do with it..." She raised her eyes blissfully toward heaven. "I bet if I tried hard enough I could just talk myself into falling in love with Eric."

"Oh, Iris! The poor man doesn't deserve such a fate."

"Really, dear, it would solve all our problems."

To her surprise Jessica saw that her sister-in-law was serious. "How would it do that?" she asked.

Iris looked at her with uncharacteristic sadness. "You know very well that you can't have Mother and me hanging about your neck for the rest of your life."

Jessica hurried over to her and embraced her. "Don't ever say such a thing! How can you? You're my family and we're sticking together. Of course you're not hanging about my neck, unless you think I was hanging about yours those years when the going was good!"

Iris seemed somewhat consoled by her words. "All the same, it's not a bad idea."

"But you can't be serious!" Jessica exclaimed. "You've known Eric all your life. You can't just make yourself fall in love with him. Why, you used to throw mud pies at him and torment him all the time, you told me so yourself. Do you think that's a sound basis for romance?"

A gleefully sly look returned to Iris's eyes. "That's just it. I've bullied him all my life, so I know I'll make a great wife for him!"

Jessica joined in her laughter. "And what do you suppose poor Eric would have to say to all this?"

"Well, the idea hasn't occurred to him yet—it only occurred to me this morning—but once I've helped him to think of it, I think he just might like it."

The doorbell rang for the second time that morning, and Iris ran to answer it. A minute later she was back with three beribboned cellophane boxes in her arms.

"Take a look at these!" she cried excitedly. "They're from our new neighbor thanking us for dinner. Gardenias for mother, orchids for me and, oh look, the most beautiful red roses for you."

Two days later Jessica was returning home from the Phillipses' farm, where she had spent the morning riding, when she saw a familiar Jeep parked by the side of the road leading to the quarry. It was the same road on which she had met the Jeep's owner for the first time. She pulled up beside it, but saw no one. She hesitated for a moment, then drove on. A little further on she stopped again. A tiny conflict of wills took place—her will to keep going, and an irresistible force that urged her to stop and look for him. She drove the car back and parked it near his, got out, and followed a narrow track that led from the road into the bush.

It was a cool day, and Jessica was dressed warmly in a pair of old jodhpurs, a white shirt, and a rust-colored tweed jacket. Stones crunched loudly under her riding boots, making the only sound in the quiet, overcast afternoon. She walked some distance before she saw the opening to the quarry. There was no one there, and she kept walking. Suddenly, after a sharp turn in the track, she saw him a few yards before her. He had climbed an outcrop of rocks and was chipping at its surface with a small hammer. His back was to her.

Jessica froze in her tracks. Now that he was so close she was reluctant to speak to him. She was about to turn back when he looked around and saw her. She knew he couldn't have seen her approach, but he had turned almost as if he had expected to see her there.

"I saw your Jeep parked by the road," Jessica said. "I came to thank you for the beautiful flowers—on all our behalfs." She realized that her reason sounded a little lame, her explanation a little too eager.

"You're welcome," he said. He nodded at her clothes. "Been riding?"

"Yes, at the Phillipses' farm."

"Why don't you come to mine? It's much closer," he invited.

"Oh, have you bought horses?" she asked with interest. Riding was one of her greatest joys, but her two horses had been sold off along with everything else.

Peter Savage jumped off the rock, landing almost at her feet. "Not yet, but I will if you come over to ride them," he said, looking down at her. As always Jessica found his nearness overwhelming.

A warning rumble sounded in the sky above.

"I think it's going to rain," Jessica said unnecessarily, glancing up at the sky. Savage didn't reply but stood looking down at her. She had noticed before that he was one of those rare people who was not made uncomfortable by silence. But *she* felt disconcerted and jittery. There was something too intimate about his silences.

Now she searched nervously for something to say.

"Have you settled into Rom—into your new home yet?" she asked.

"Why don't you come over to see?" he invited again.

"Oh, no," Jessica said—too hastily, she realized at once.

He looked at her with curiosity. "Do you resent me so much for having bought the place?"

"No, of course not," she protested. "Why would I? Someone had to."

He looked at her for a long moment. "I feel as if you do, as if that resentment will always be between us." When she didn't answer, he went on. "But don't forget I didn't know you or anything about you when I bought it."

"Are you saying that if you *had* known, you wouldn't have bought it?" she challenged.

"No," he admitted and laughed. "I would have bought it a whole lot sooner."

Suddenly large drops of rain began to fall. Jessica turned to go, but he took her arm and pulled her back.

"You'll never make it without getting soaked to the skin. This is going to be a hell of a storm."

As if on cue, the rain began to fall in a heavy, icy sheet. Jessica gasped at the sudden drenching. He turned and ran, pulling her after him. Stumbling over the uneven ground, Jessica followed him blindly. They took shelter in a shallow cave under an outcropping of rock. Already they were soaked. Water streamed from Jessica's hair, and Peter's shirt was plastered to his chest. He pulled a large, still-dry handkerchief from his jeans pocket and, taking her chin in his hand, wiped her face and hair, then his own. She began to shiver.

"If I'd known you were coming, I'd have laid a fire," he joked. Then, seeing her shiver more violently, he reached over to pull her to him.

"No!" The word came out as an alarmed shout, much louder than she had intended, and she stepped back out of his reach. Peter turned his piercing blue eyes on her, and his mouth drew down in what she was sure was an expression of scorn.

"Don't worry," he said quietly, as if her alarm had been caused by something else, "it won't last long. Just a flash storm."

Jessica huddled in a corner of the small cave, deeply mortified. She had never in her life been so unnerved by a man. Even as a teenager she had handled men with cool self-possession. Now, a grown woman, she was shrinking from Savage's touch like a flittery old maid. But there was something in her powerful physical awareness of him that she found very threatening. Even worse, she had let him see it. She would have done anything to unsay that "no."

A sudden gust of wind drove the rain into her corner, and when Peter reached over for her once more, firmly this time, she did not recoil.

"There, get behind me," he said, pulling her to him and turning his back to her so that he sat facing the cave's opening, shielding her from the torrent. Jessica's legs were folded under her, her knees pressing into the small of his back. There wasn't an inch to move in in the cramped space, and she felt his back burning her even through his damp shirt. She stared at his wide shoulders, his hair, darkened and curled with dampness, the sunburned skin on the back of his neck. Every inch of her was aware of his closeness. She shivered again and wondered how it was possible to be cold and burning at the same time.

"If you catch cold," he warned, half turning to look at her, "it won't be for lack of me trying to prevent it."

"I won't catch cold," she replied, and immediately a loud sneeze belied her words.

"Are you sure you wouldn't rather try my cold-prevention methods?" he pressed with a glint in his eyes.

"Quite sure!" she told him.

He shrugged. "It's your loss—to say nothing of mine."

Jessica ignored him and began to talk to prevent them

from lapsing into another uncomfortable silence. She asked him about the time he had worked in this same quarry and, relieved to be back on a safe subject, listened to his tales as avidly as if sandstone mining had been her lifelong interest.

In a quarter of an hour the rain stopped as abruptly as it had begun.

"No need to ask how relieved *you* are." He smiled down at her. "As for me, I'm a convert to the belief that 'with each rain some good must fall.' I don't know when I've enjoyed a half hour more."

Jessica, trying to struggle to her feet, gasped out in sudden pain. "Aaah! My legs have gone to sleep. I can't move."

In an instant he was kneeling beside her, taking her gently by the arm. "Slowly, slowly. Lean on me."

Painfully, Jessica stretched her legs and, with his support, rose to her knees until they were both kneeling face-to-face. As their eyes met, the concern in his changed swiftly to something else that made Jessica stare back at him as if hypnotized. Then his mouth was on hers, and she felt a hollow plunge inside as if all will and strength had been drawn from her by the impact of his lips on hers. She yielded helplessly and completely to his kiss.

She felt his hands, those powerful, rough hands that held such fascination for her, trace a searing trail up along her throat until they held her face captive. He drew away from her to look searchingly into her eyes before his mouth came down once more to burn hotly on her eyelids, her neck, and her lips again. Each time he sought a new spot he looked at her expectantly as if waiting for something, as if it wasn't enough. She found his gazes more unbearably intimate than the touch of his lips, and to escape their intensity she clasped her arms about his neck to draw his mouth back to hers. At once something loosened in him, and she knew that this was what he had been waiting for. Yielding to his passion had not been enough. He wanted her to return it.

The increased, demanding pressure of his mouth made her strain against him in an uncontrollable response. The hard ground bit painfully into her knees, but the pain was easy to ignore compared with the stronger sensation of desire that was welling up inside her.

His hands slid under her jacket, under the shirt that had come loose, caressing the bare skin of her back with ever increasing pressure, then drawing her closer with a gesture so full of urgency it stirred the beginnings of panic in her. The panic grew until, with a gasp, she drew away.

The flush of desire still burning in her cheeks, she looked at him dazedly, a look that slowly changed to incredulous horror. What had happened? How had she lost control... How could she have yielded... responded the way she had? And to him of all men!

She jumped up and, disregarding the still-weak legs that threatened to give way under her, stumbled past him out of the cave. In a few moments he had caught up with her and, seizing her arm, whirled her around.

His eyes glittered with anger, but when he saw the dismay in hers, they softened.

"You look as if you've just been reminded against your will that you're human, too," he said almost gently. "But don't expect any apologies. I'm glad I'm the one who reminded you."

chapter 6

THE "LILAC BALL" was a deceptively lighthearted and pastoral name for what was in fact one of the most formal and exclusive social events in the entire state of New South Wales.

Residence in Sommerville or its surrounding area alone did not guarantee an invitation. That was left entirely to the discretion of the ball committee, headed by Marjorie Cunningham, who handpicked the five hundred guests. The inclusion of families like the Romneys and Cuttlers was automatic, as was the exclusion of many others. Newcomers to the area sometimes found themselves waiting several years to be invited.

The week before the ball, toward the end of October, was an especially trying one for Jessica. Carlotta had plunged into such low spirits that it was impossible to cheer her up. This would be the first year since the Romneys had settled in Sommerville that they would not be at the center of the activities that accompanied the ball.

In previous years Romney House had served as a focal point for all activities. Invitations to dinners, dances, cocktails, and picnics had been as sought-after as for the ball itself. In the week before the ball the guest rooms had been filled to capacity, the kitchen stoves never cooled, the noise of festivity never died down. Romney House had played host to guests from all over the country, from abroad, and on occasion even to royalty. This week before the ball the three women really felt their loss, especially Carlotta.

Trying to cheer her up was a full-time job for Jessica, whose usual self-possession was undergoing a severe trial. In the long months since Roderick's death she had been able to put one disaster after another firmly behind her and get on with the business of surviving. But she had always had pride and self-esteem to see her through, and since the incident with Peter Savage, she felt the loss of both. That she had allowed a man she disliked so much to kiss her—and not only let him, but kissed him back with fervor—still did not seem possible to her. That she had given herself over to such a purely physical reaction was unthinkable. And more than a kiss was at stake; it was their whole relationship. She had drawn the line between them so carefully, then overstepped it herself.

The thought of meeting Peter Savage again was a constant fear, but she could not avoid it. She knew he would be at the ball, and she would just have to resign herself to the meeting. She would have given anything not to have to go, but she'd had such a hard time convincing Carlotta to attend she couldn't beg off herself. The Romneys *always* attended, and this year it was more important than ever that they do so.

The ball was held in the Sommerville Town Hall, an imposing though overly ornate Victorian building. Its wood-paneled chambers were emptied of all furniture, and its connecting doors opened to form a vast hall in which the dancing took place. Outside on the grounds several tents were set up for refreshments, and all the trees were hung with dimly glowing Chinese lanterns.

When the first Lilac Ball had been held, more than 150 years before, it had been a local affair attended by all and sundry, from farm laborers and landed gentry to the village residents. It had been a folksy celebration of the coming of spring, the blossoming of flowers—in particular the beautiful white and purple lilacs for which the district was famous. There had been traditional Australian bush barbecues with sides of sheep and homemade sausages cooked over open fires, and damper, a native bread made from unleavened dough, cooked in the ashes. Barrels of beer and homemade cakes and fruit pies had completed the fare.

Now, though some of the original dishes were still served for a touch of quaintness, they were eclipsed by more sophisticated food such as lobster mousse and bombes of various kinds. More champagne than beer flowed. The music was no longer supplied by the local fiddler and his accompanists but by a band flown in from Sydney.

Hundreds of guests, champagne glasses in hand, were already trampling the lawns when the Romneys and Cutlers arrived together in two cars. A local television crew and several society reporters from the city newspapers were stalking the more decorative and distinguished guests. The Romneys qualified as both, and when they emerged from their cars, flashbulbs began to pop. Jessica disliked this part intensely, and she lingered in the background while Carlotta and Iris flashed poised and practiced smiles in the direction of the cameras.

Eric took a proprietary hold of Jessica's arm and propelled her toward the entrance. On the way he kept spotting important businessmen and prominent politicians to whom he just "had to say a quick hallo," so that it took almost half an hour to reach the ballroom. All this time Jessica stood by his side smiling politely, listening to the same half-dozen meaningless observations over and over again. The evening stretched drearily and interminably before her. She was unconscious of the admiring glances she attracted even in that crowd of fashionably and expensively dressed men and women. She wore a dream of a dress in pink silk and fragile silver lace netting. Her hair was parted at the center and drawn softly away from her temples to form a gentle coil at the nape of her neck and fastened with a small antique amethyst-and-diamond star. Around her wrists she wore two diamond-and-amethyst bracelets. A pair of dainty silver slippers matched her silver mesh evening purse.

The admiration directed at her was not lost on Eric, whose chest seemed to swell and whose hold on her became more and more possessive. As she stood next to him making polite conversation, she was conscious of a nervous expectation in the pit of her stomach.

At last they reached the ballroom, where the dancing had already begun, having been officially opened earlier by a representative of the governor. At once Eric swept her onto the floor. He was a smooth and graceful dancer and moved her expertly around the room.

The next dance was claimed by Colonel Phillips, who danced rather as he rode, recklessly charging about with her, coming perilously close to other couples on the floor. It took Jessica all her skill to steer them away from countless near collisions. The partners she had for the next two dances were not much better, and she was relieved when the band finally stopped for a short interval.

She tried not to wonder if he was there, if he was watching her. When the next round of dances began and she still hadn't seen him, she began to hope that in the crush of five hundred people she might just possibly avoid him all evening.

But when, almost an hour later, she looked up and saw him approaching her, the sight of him was like a long-awaited blow. She almost reeled under the impact. Blood rushed to her face as he came purposefully toward her, looking to neither left nor right, as if no one else in the room existed. She had willed herself to act composed by the time he reached her.

"Good evening," he said, taking a hand she had not extended.

She sought for something commonplace to say. "Are you enjoying the ball?" she asked.

"I'm only just beginning to," he said meaningfully. He glanced about the room and added, "But I'm inclined to agree with your sister-in-law. It's not the most jolly bash-up I've ever been to."

Beyond Pride

Jessica bristled at once. "A little too provincial for your liking, Mr. Savage?" she asked sarcastically.

"I don't quite see its purpose. For a start there's not a lilac in sight. For another everyone looks kind of grim, as if the whole affair was a duty. What's the point?"

Jessica, who regarded the ball in much the same light, nevertheless felt annoyed by the criticism of this outsider. "The point is that we like to observe our local traditions. This one goes back a hundred and fifty years," she informed him coldly.

"Local tradition?" he repeated, looking around the room once more. "I don't see many of the local people I know frolicking about."

"Perhaps a failure on someone's part to invite the boys from the Royal Victoria," she suggested acidly. The moment the words were out she could have bitten her tongue. She had sounded downright snobbish. It wasn't as if she didn't agree with him, so why was she always so quickly provoked to oppose him? At least, she realized, her sourness had taken some of the edge off her apprehension at meeting him again.

Peter Savage threw back his head and laughed. Jessica looked about frantically. A moment ago she had been surrounded by a crowd. Now everyone had disappeared. Eric, whom she hadn't been able to pry from her side for the last hour, was nowhere to be seen.

"Will you thaw out for a moment and dance with me?" Peter asked.

"I'm sorry, I'm engaged for this dance," she lied and prayed that anyone—even Colonel Phillips—would claim her before the music began again. She was about to excuse herself to go in search of her nonexistent partner when the band launched into a new number.

"Consider yourself disengaged." He took her into his arms and led her onto the floor. "Anyone who keeps you waiting doesn't deserve a second chance. I must warn you, though, that I'm not very good at this stuff. The best I can promise is that I won't trample your feet."

By now the dance floor was crowded, and they

couldn't move much. Peter held her close, and her heart began to hammer so wildly she began to feel faint. Suddenly, with a recurring sense of helplessness, she knew how that kiss had happened. Because here in his arms she realized that if he kissed her now she would be lost again.

Peter bent his head and, putting his mouth close to her ear, whispered, "Anyone who tries to cut in now is a dead man." She could not be certain that his lips brushed her hair.

She closed her eyes and became oblivious to everything except the slow, close movement of their two bodies. They didn't exchange another word as she stayed in his arms for the next two dances. The communication between them in those moments was too strong for words. When the music stopped and they finally drew apart, Jessica blinked as if emerging from a soft mist into a too harsh light.

The end of the music and the distance between them brought back reality—and Eric. Jessica reached for his arm with the eagerness of a drowning person for a life preserver. Her gesture was not lost on Peter, whose eyes turned a colder blue and whose lips narrowed with displeasure. The two men exchanged polite greetings, Peter's eyes all the while on Jessica's hand, which was holding Eric's arm. He hesitated for a moment, then, seeming to make up his mind about something, excused himself and left.

Jessica wondered for the first time if he had brought a date with him, and the thought gave her a small, unexpected pain. Of course he would have, she decided, then couldn't help wondering if he already knew someone in Sommerville well enough to ask, or if his date was an outsider.

Suddenly she was terribly tired and wanted to go home. She wondered if she could persuade Eric to leave.

She turned to him. "I suppose you're enjoying yourself very much?"

"I certainly am," he replied warmly. "I think this

year's ball is an even bigger success than last year's."

"That's what I thought." Jessica sighed with resignation.

They danced again until they were interrupted by Iris, whom Jessica had not seen for most of the evening.

"Look over there." Iris pointed with glee. "Can you believe your eyes?"

Jessica followed her finger and saw Carlotta doing a dignified glide around the dance floor—in the arms of Peter Savage!

"No, I don't think I *can* believe it," Jessica gasped. "How did that happen?"

"He's been doing a snow job on her that would put a blizzard to shame." Iris giggled and waved a glass brimming with champagne. "She's done her best to be hoity with him all evening, but he refuses to be daunted. He just treats her as if she were the sweetest old thing. I think sooner or later he'll succeed in winning her over."

"Why would he bother?" Jessica mused.

"I wonder," Iris said dryly, giving her sister-in-law a significant look.

"I think the man's trying to ingratiate himself socially. He knows that doing it through Carlotta is the right way," Eric suggested sourly.

"Oh, Eric, you *are* a dunce sometimes!" Iris exclaimed, tugging impatiently at his arm. "Half the women in Sommerville are potty about him already. In case you haven't been watching, they're lining up to dance with him. He hasn't had to lift a finger to ingratiate himself. Now come on, darling, you haven't danced with me all evening, and I have sooo much to talk to you about." With a conspiratorial wink at Jessica, she led him away.

Later, when the Cuttlers and the Romneys were taking refreshment together in one of the tents, Jessica saw Peter Savage again, surrounded by a bevy of the prettiest girls, bending attentively to their animated conversation. Even from a distance the flush of admiration on their faces was clearly visible.

"A good thing he came stag," Iris said in a wry aside

to Jessica some time later. "Can you imagine how a date would cope with all that competition?" She seemed to expect some reaction to this comment but received none.

Just then Peter looked in their direction and, much to Jessica's chagrin, caught them staring at him. That secret smile that she found so insufferable appeared on his face. He said a few words to his companions before coming over to join them.

"You seem to have found your own painless method for getting through the evening," Iris observed archly, gesturing toward the group of young women he had just left.

"A man must seek solace where he can," he answered, looking straight at Jessica.

She deliberately misunderstood his meaning. "And Mr. Savage needs all the solace he can get," she told Iris. "He was complaining to me earlier how bored he was by our stuffy little affair."

Before Peter could reply they were joined by several others, and for a while the matter was dropped. As soon as she could, Jessica slipped away to take a stroll around the almost deserted grounds. Most of the guests were inside the tents eating supper, and everything outside was silent. The cool air felt good after the hot, crowded tents. Jessica had hardly sat down on a garden bench when she heard footsteps approaching.

He stood before her, an overhead lantern casting a silvery light on his hair but throwing his face into shadow. Only the intense blueness of his eyes was clearly visible.

"I'm sorry if my remarks about the ball annoyed you," he said in a soft, low voice.

"What annoys me, Mr. Savage, is your constant implication that we—me in particular—are a bunch of snobs."

"Some of you—not you in particular—are," he replied, and though she could not see his face, she knew from his voice that he was laughing.

"Then I think you might have made a mistake in picking Sommerville to settle down in," she said frigidly.

"I don't think so."

"You seem to find everything about it vastly amusing," she pursued.

He laughed softly. "You know what you are? A chauvinist. A true-blue, or in this case fair dinkum, chauvinist. It's hard to believe you've only lived here a few years.... No, I like the place, and I'm going to make my home here. But there are some things I'm at odds with and always will be. Shindigs like this are one of them. I have a feeling we're all here because it's the 'done thing.' Nothing holds less appeal for me than the 'done thing.' And by the way, I couldn't help noticing—having closely watched you all night—that you weren't exactly overwhelmed by excitement yourself. So why get so huffy about it with me?"

Jessica wasn't certain what caused her to flush—his revelation that he had been watching her or the way he was speaking.

Anger put a sarcastic edge to her voice. "And I can't help noticing that, despite your democratic views, you've bought the biggest, most prestigious property this side of Sydney," she threw at him.

For a moment he was silent, and she wondered if she had gone too far. Oh, why did she keep defending principles she didn't believe in?

When he finally spoke his voice betrayed no sign that she had insulted him. "Make no mistake about it, I have nothing against money or the things it can buy. I've fought hard enough for it all my life to appreciate it. I just don't like it when people think it makes them superior to those who don't have it. They form clubs and hold affairs like this to prove it. Now, let's both get off our soapboxes and go for a stroll. I wanted to ask—"

"Jessica, Jessica are you out there?"

Peter muttered an uncomplimentary word as Eric's voice drew nearer. "That bloke's got timing like a two-bob watch," he growled.

"Jessica, I've been looking—" Eric stopped in his tracks when he saw them. "Oh, here you are." He gave

Peter an unfriendly look and said to her, "The band's about to start up again. I came to get you before the floor got too crowded."

"I'd love to." Jessica jumped up, taking his proffered arm. "Excuse us, won't you?" she said to Peter over her shoulder. "You'll probably want to leave this shindig early anyway, won't you?" His face was still in the shadows, and she couldn't see the expression on it. What had he wanted to ask her? The question nagged persistently at her, even when she was on the dance floor with Eric.

Something told her Eric's mind wasn't wholly on their dancing, either, and he soon confirmed her suspicion when he said a little nervously, "Do you mind if we sit this one out? Actually there was something...that is...could we talk?"

An uneasy feeling started to grow in Jessica as they left the floor and headed for a small, deserted room on the other side of the hall. Once inside, Eric carefully closed the door and offered her a chair. Jessica sat down, feeling more uneasy than ever.

Eric began pacing the floor, obviously finding it hard to begin. He cleared his throat several times. Jessica braced herself.

"Jessica, I've known you for several years now and...well, you must be aware of how much...how I admire you."

Immediately she felt a great pang of guilt. Her recent behavior had precipitated this declaration. She had never actually said anything, never actually encouraged him that way, she tried to excuse herself, but she knew she had been guilty of misleading him with insincere attention. And all for her own selfish ends.

"Oh, Eric—" she began to protest, but he cut her off.

"I'm a very cautious man. I like to look thoroughly before I leap. I like to know before I commit myself...."

Despite her trepidation of what was about to come, Jessica had to stifle a smile. Eric managed to make the whole thing sound as if he was testing the ground for a business merger.

Beyond Pride

"I wanted to get some idea...well." Suddenly he took a deep breath and plunged. "Could you ever feel anything more for me than friendship?"

"Eric, dear." Jessica put her hand gently on his arm. "I'm so very flattered and so grateful for everything you've done for us. You've been a dear friend, the best there is." She paused for a moment, dreading to hurt him and cursing her selfish stupidity. "I knew you when Roderick...because you were his best friend...don't you see, it would be impossible," she pleaded, her eyes filling with tears.

Eric looked at her with a mixture of disappointment and gratitude. Using his friendship with Roderick and the associations it would always hold for her as an excuse had helped save his pride.

"I understand." He smiled and pressed her hand. Together they went to the door arm in arm. He opened it and stepped aside for her, then detained her by taking both her hands in his.

"I hope that this has done nothing to jeopardize our friendship," he said.

In reply Jessica leaned over and gave him a gentle kiss. As she turned from the door, her eyes met the cold, hard stare of Peter Savage.

chapter 7

"JESSICA, JESSICA DEAR!" Carlotta's voice called fretfully from the cool shelter of the veranda. "I simply won't allow you to stay out there any longer. Your skin will be completely ruined."

Jessica straightened and put a hand to her aching back. "I won't be long," she called back, concealing the fatigue from her voice. "I just want to finish this section of the walk."

She was laying old, handmade bricks to pave a walk through the grass to the front entrance. There was no other approach to the house, and every time it rained visitors sank ankle deep in mud. When a small outbuilding had been demolished at the back of the garden, Jessica had saved the bricks for just this purpose. With restoration work going on in every part of Australia, everything old and original was highly prized, and these bricks, made with convict labor more than a century before, were worth a small fortune. She had meant to do them justice by hiring a professional man to do the job, but the unexpected expense of having to rewire a section of the house had cropped up, and there was not enough money for both. Would there never be an end to these hitches that played havoc with her carefully laid plans and budget? she wondered with frustration.

Jessica had been working for two hours, and only sheer willpower kept her going. Even through the thick leather gloves she wore she could feel the bricks grazing her palms, and she had to keep her teeth gritted against the pain in her back. Her wide-brimmed hat kept the sun off her face and shoulders, but it did nothing to ward off the intense heat of the afternoon. It was an unseasonably hot November day, and rain earlier in the week had made the air heavy with humidity.

Carlotta's anxious fussing finally had its effect. Straightening with a grimace of pain, Jessica took off her hat and drew off her heavy gloves. Slipping out of her sandals, she turned on the garden tap and let the water run over her feet, splashing some on her flushed face and on the back of her neck. In the shade of the veranda she sank into a deeply cushioned wicker chair and fanned herself with a magazine, relishing the cool touch of the marble flagging under her bare feet. She wore a loose, light peasant blouse and a floral print skirt, which she hitched over her knees as she sat sprawled in the chair.

Iris appeared with a tray, bearing tall glasses and a jug that tinkled with the sound of ice cubes.

"What I'd give to be able to dive into our pool now." She sighed deeply and poured out glasses of lemonade.

"I don't think you used the pool more than twice in all the time I lived there," Jessica said wearily, cooling her brow with her icy glass.

"Maybe not," Iris conceded, "but just knowing it was there if I wanted it made me feel cooler." She looked at Jessica closely and exclaimed guiltily, "Oh, Jessica! You look so hot and worn out, and here I am whining about how much I miss the pool."

"And no wonder," Carlotta cut in, from the chair next to them, "working like a coolie in that sun. I won't have you driving yourself like that, darling. Surely we can afford a—"

"I'm fine, really," Jessica hastened to assure them, anxious to ward off a discussion of finances right then. "The work's not hard at all," she lied. "As soon as I've cooled off a bit I can just about finish it." Secretly she

Beyond Pride

stole a dismayed glance at the path. It didn't look nearly as neat as she'd hoped.

"I won't hear of it!" Carlotta declared.

"Why don't you let him help, Jessica? He has offered to so many times," Iris said with a searching look.

Jessica didn't have to ask who "he" was. "Because we don't need anyone's help," she replied, setting her mouth in a stubborn line.

"Then I'll help you myself," Iris said, making it sound like a threat.

Jessica gave her an affectionate smile as she tried to conjure up a picture of Iris laying bricks. "You're doing all you can already. You're hardly out of the kitchen. Now let's not fuss about it anymore," she pleaded.

Iris shook her head in despair, but changed the subject.

Drowsily Jessica half listened to the others' chatter. Yes, Peter Savage had renewed his offer of help several times, but she had always refused it. Despite that one slip in the quarry, she was still determined to keep a distance between them. In the few weeks since she had known him he had somehow managed to intrude into her life in a way she resented. She found herself thinking, feeling, and doing things she had never done before.

The phrase he had used in the quarry—that she had "just been reminded that she was human, too"—kept taunting her. She didn't need a man like Peter Savage to remind her that she was human. Certainly she didn't need *his* way of reminding her!

Why he went out of his way to find her, only to end each encounter in a derisive argument, puzzled her. He certainly wasn't motivated by the same reasons as other men who had approached her. He never flirted, wasn't given to flattery, and even when he did pay a rare compliment, he made it sound more like a direct, matter-of-fact statement than praise aimed to please. Altogether he was a puzzling man whose actions and words could contradict each other in rapid succession, jumping perplexingly from harsh sarcasm to gentle concern to arrogant self-assurance.

Nothing was more puzzling than the curious way he had looked at her when he'd witnessed her kiss with Eric. They had not exchanged a word, but his cold blue stare had stayed with her. She stirred impatiently in her chair. There she was again, wasting her thoughts on him! She forced her mind back to the conversation going on around her.

"—and I heard Marjorie tell the Phillipses that he's had a large crew working around the clock for the past two weeks. He seems to be giving the old place a thorough going-over," Iris was saying. Suddenly she stopped abruptly, peered into the garden, and announced in a hurried whisper, "And speaking of Romney House, here comes the master himself."

Jessica's eyes flew open to see Peter Savage approaching with long, unhurried strides. Her first impulse was to jump up and rush inside to fix her disheveled appearance, but she reminded herself that he didn't warrant the effort and settled for adjusting her skirt down over her knees. There was nothing she could do, however, to adjust the beat of her heart to a calmer tempo.

Springing onto the veranda with a light step, Peter included them all in a friendly greeting. Looking freshly showered and cool in a pair of tan cotton slacks and open-necked tan shirt, he accepted the seat and glass of lemonade Iris offered.

"I expect it's much cooler up at the big house," Carlotta commented, giving him a resentful stare.

He agreed that it was a wonderfully cool house.

Carlotta sighed and waved a small ivory fan. "This place is a hellhole—but then what can you expect in such tiny, cramped quarters," she complained, managing to sound as if she were addressing a heartless landlord who had dispossessed them. Jessica winced with embarrassment. When would Carlotta ever get over the notion that he was somehow responsible for the loss of their home?

"You used to complain as much about the heat at the big house, as I recall," Iris said without sympathy. "Not

Beyond Pride

to mention the cold, the damp, and the leaking roof."

"Any time you feel uncomfortable here, you're welcome to make use of the big house," Peter offered. "As a matter of fact, I came over to ask if you ladies would like to take a swim. The pool has just been cleaned and refilled."

"We're planning to have our own pool built," Carlotta said, rejecting his offer haughtily.

"Are you? Let me know when," he responded pleasantly, still unperturbed by her rudeness. "I have a subsidiary company that builds pools. I'll be glad to help."

Jessica almost liked him at that moment for refusing to take offense. It was as if what Iris had said was true, that he was trying to win Carlotta over. She met her sister-in-law's eyes and was given an "I told you so" look. She glanced quickly away.

The telephone rang, and Iris went to answer it. "It's for you, Mother!" she called a moment later. Carlotta went inside, leaving Peter and Jessica alone.

Peter sat with his legs stretched out before him, his arms crossed comfortably over his head. Since his arrival he hadn't looked at Jessica.

Jessica, becoming fidgety as she always did during one of his intense silences, picked up the jug of lemonade and dropped it at once with an involuntary gasp of pain. Some of the liquid had spilled onto her hand, and the acid lemonade burned into an open, bloody gash on her palm.

She tried to hide her hand, but in one quick step he was beside her, kneeling by her chair. He took the hand forcibly and looked at it, then reached for the other one and studied that, too.

The hours Jessica had spent digging in the garden, attempting some carpentry work, and carrying bricks had taken their toll on her hands. Her palms were crisscrossed with calluses, scratches, and a couple of deep cuts.

Peter's voice was tight when he spoke at last. "What the hell have you been doing to make them like this?"

"Just a little work around the house," Jessica replied

in a faint voice, overwhelmingly conscious of his fair head bent so closely over her lap, his thumbs stroking the bruises on her palms. Her fingers looked helplessly captive in his own strong hands. It was all very well, she thought, staring at his gold hair, to decide to keep her distance when he wasn't there, but when he was as close as this... No, she wouldn't give in to that again.

She tried to pull her hands away, but he looked up with a frown on his face. "Of course it would kill you to ask me for help."

"I don't need help," she said stubbornly, looking away.

"Don't play Scarlett O'Hara with me!" he suddenly exploded. "This whole act of keeping the ol' plantation going all by your li'l ol' self is just so much bloody— You silly woman, you'd rather break your back than bend your pride a little."

Jessica wrenched her hands away and jumped up from her chair. "It might be an act to you, but it happens to be the way we stay alive," she cried, her green eyes blazing.

"It doesn't have to be that way if you'll only take the help that's yours for the asking," he countered, leaning closer to make his point.

Jessica drew back. "I can't seem to make you understand, no matter how much I try, that I do not need your help!" she said in a voice trembling with indignation.

"You need it, all right, Jessica, you just won't take it." He shot her a piercing look, then, shaking his head, walked to the other side of the veranda.

Through her anger at his scornful words and his interference, she was acutely aware that for the first time he had called her by her first name. The word sounded almost caressing after the mocking emphasis he usually laid on "Mrs. Romney."

After a few moments' silence he returned to her side. "I don't suppose you reject offers of help from Eric Cuttler," he accused with a glare.

Beyond Pride

The vehemence in his voice brought her head up in surprise. "That's quite different. He's an old and trusted friend," she replied stiffly.

"That much I could see for myself the other night," Peter said grimly, turning away and beginning to pace the veranda.

Jessica stared after him in amazement. What was it about Eric that had made him lose his usually unflappable composure? First that cold glare at the ball, and now this. That the two men didn't get on had been obvious from the start, but Peter had always treated Eric as something of a joke. Now he suddenly seemed angered by the very mention of his name.

Peter continued to pace up and down for a while longer before coming back to face her. In a gesture of frustration he ran his fingers through his hair and gave her a sudden, disarming smile. "You've put me in rather a spot, you know," he confided. "It so happens that I've come over especially to ask for *your* help."

"*My* help?" she repeated, mystified. "With what?"

He thrust his hands in his pocket and, leaning against the veranda railing, began with a wry grimace. "It seems certain things are expected of me—certain things that go with the ownership of Romney House. I was given the hint by Miss Cunningham, who paid me a long visit yesterday. She tells me one of these obligations involves—God help me—a flower show and fete, or some such thing, that has apparently always been held on the grounds of Romney House. She let me know that if I didn't host it this year I'd be tampering with historic tradition."

Jessica gave him an exaggerated look of wonder. "You don't mean to say you've let her bully you into doing something just because it's the 'done thing'?"

"If I give you a few minutes to rub my nose in it, can I go on?" he inquired patiently.

"Go on," Jessica invited, crossing her arms expectantly.

He gave her a sideways glance and continued. "Whatever the damned thing is, it's completely out of my range of experience."

"I didn't think anything was," she commented, but he ignored her.

"The closest I've ever come to throwing a bash on that scale was a certain memorable bucks' night I held for one of my mates. I don't think duplicating that event is what the lady has in mind."

"No," Jessica agreed. "But I'm still reeling with amazement that you'd consider overcoming your contempt for one of our quaint local customs," she insisted.

"Oh, but I approve of this one," he said. "First, everyone is invited—that sold me straight away. Second, it's for charity."

"You're in a very charitable mood today," Jessica observed sweetly. "First me, now the people of the town. You're becoming a regular patron of widows and orphans, aren't you?"

"Widows in particular," he agreed audaciously.

She grimaced and asked, "What sort of help do you want from me?"

"To organize the thing."

"Any number of people in town can do that," she pointed out.

"I'm asking you."

She found it difficult to reject such a direct plea. It would be downright ungracious to turn him down after all his offers of help, from whatever motive he'd made them. But she wanted to stay away from him and from Romney House. She felt cornered.

"I really don't see why you need my help at all," she began tentatively. "The whole thing is a simple matter of opening your grounds to the public. They'll do the rest. You'll find the foldaway tables, benches, and chairs we've always used still in that small annex next to the stables. The local carpenter will help you set up the booths. You'll have to provide most of the glasses, cutlery, and decorations, but you'll find stacks of them on the back shelves of the china pantry. Apart from that you'll only have to coordinate the flower show—probably judge it, too—and make sure the women don't make more sponge cakes than we can sell, because last year everyone—"

She was stopped by a loud, agonized groan. "The whole thing might be a simple matter to *you*," he said, "but I don't know the difference between a sponge cake and a Christmas pudding, and as for judging a flower show . . . !"

She turned away to hide a smile at his expression. "Keep that look of helpless terror on your face and any number of women will rush to help you," she advised.

"Just you will do."

"Well, I—"

"Unless you don't want to because it would mean you'd have to come over to the big house," he challenged, looking closely to see her reaction.

"Of course not," she almost snapped. "I told you before that has nothing . . . oh, all right! I'll help." The man was certainly adept at setting and springing traps, she told herself grimly. She had just committed herself to spending hours in his company when only a little while before she had made up her mind to have as little contact with him as possible.

"Thank you," he said simply, turning from her to look out at the garden. When his eyes moved to the uneven, rather messy result of her afternoon's labor, he frowned. In the next moment he had started unbuttoning his shirt, and with one swift movement pulled it off his back.

"What are you doing?" Jessica demanded in alarm.

"Those bricks." He nodded toward them. "They're laid all wrong—going to sink into the ground every which way. I'm going to fix them."

"That's not necessary," she protested. "If you show me how to lay them properly, I'll do them myself."

"It took me several months to become a good bricklayer. I don't think I can teach you the trade in one afternoon. Besides," he added, looking back at her, "one good turn deserves another."

Without another word he began pulling up the bricks she had so laboriously laid earlier that day. Her eyes became riveted to his bare, broad back, which shone golden-brown in the sun. She watched the play of muscles in his arms and neck as he stacked the bricks. Not a motion was wasted. He did everything with the practiced ease and economy of an athlete.

Against her will Jessica's eyes were drawn back to him again and again, held there by the memory of those powerful arms about her in the quarry and on the dance floor, the gentle, caressing touch of those strong hands. She despised herself for these thoughts but could not shut them out.

She stirred guiltily when Iris appeared beside her.

"My word!" Iris let out a low whistle of appreciation as she took in the half-naked body of their guest.

Jessica nudged her in the side and hissed a warning "shh."

"I was only admiring the wonderful...work he's doing," Iris responded in a ribald whisper. Jessica shook her head, smiling. Iris was one of those rare women to whom an occasional vulgarity was becoming. "What's he doing, anyway?"

"Showing me what a lousy bricklayer I am," Jessica told her.

"Hmm. Is that what he's doing?" Iris mused, unconvinced. She looked from Peter to Jessica and back to Peter again speculatively. Putting a great deal of regret in her voice, she observed, "A pity you can't stand him." And flashing her sister-in-law a wicked smile, she disappeared into the house.

Peter worked until late that afternoon. The path took orderly shape under his skilled hands. When he finished he had a quick wash under the garden tap and, putting his shirt back on, joined the three women for a late tea they had spread on a wicker table in a corner of the veranda.

An evening breeze dispersed the heat of the day,

fanning the veranda and bringing with it the fragrance of the garden. Several rosella parrots, their red and green colors vivid in the waning light, came to feed off the berries of some bushes. When Jessica threw them cake crumbs, they made shrieking dives to retrieve them.

"Tea for you, Mr. Savage, or would you rather have a beer?" Carlotta asked, pausing in the act of pouring from a silver pot.

"Tea, please."

"Are you sure? It's no trouble to get you something else if you prefer."

Iris and Jessica exchanged astonished looks. Carlotta was being extremely civil, even solicitous. She had watched his progress all afternoon without comment. Perhaps this was her way of thanking him.

Peter assured her of his preference for tea, and she handed him a cup that looked absurdly fragile in his hands. He sat with his long legs sprawled out in front of him, appearing comfortable and relaxed. Jessica felt a sudden burst of blissful tranquillity that she attributed to the loveliness of this, her favorite part of the day. For the first time in Peter's presence, she enjoyed the companionable silence that settled over all of them.

"Jessica, dear," Carlotta called to her, breaking the silence, "why don't you play that Beethoven sonata I like so much? I always think it was especially written to be played at this time of evening."

"Heavens, no," Jessica said. "I haven't played for so long my fingers would creak like rusty hinges—not to mention the piano, which hasn't been tuned in over a year."

Peter looked up with interest. "Please play," he insisted.

She shook her head. "I told you, I'm terribly out of practice."

"It won't make any difference to me, I'm tone-deaf," he confessed. When Iris joined in their plea, Jessica had no choice but to comply.

She went inside and lifted the lid of the piano, which

for a long time now had only been opened for the purpose of dusting. Once she had played almost every day, sometimes for hours at a time, but during these busy days playing the piano was one of her hobbies that had slipped into neglect. She ran tentative fingers over the keys. Her fingers felt stiff and a little insensitive from the rough work they had performed lately, but the piano was in surprisingly good tune.

Jessica began with the "Moonlight Sonata," a favorite of Carlotta's, whose taste in music was limited to the most sentimental. At first the notes came awkwardly, but she had played the piece so many times that it flowed almost automatically once she relaxed. The bittersweet, haunting melody that so many years of popularity had failed to make trite floated through the French doors to the veranda, where it was received in entranced silence.

After the sonata Jessica played a Chopin prelude, then followed it with a Mozart minuet. As always she became completely engrossed in the music, and she started with surprise when she looked up to find Peter standing next to the piano, looking down at her hands, seemingly as fascinated by them as she always was by his. She stopped abruptly, her hands sliding into her lap.

"Go on," he urged. "It's very beautiful."

"You're tone-deaf," she reminded him.

He reached for one of her hands and lifted it to examine it as he had done earlier in the afternoon. "I hear well enough to know that these are wasted laying bricks." Their eyes locked, and Jessica experienced the same suffocating sensation that had left her so powerless in the quarry.

"That's enough for tonight," she said, glancing away and freeing her hand. She shut the lid firmly.

They returned to the veranda, where Peter pulled his chair closer to hers and asked in a low voice, "Are you doing anything tonight?"

Before she could reply, footsteps approached from the garden.

"Good evening everyone," Eric said, coming up the steps.

Jessica stole an uneasy glance at the man sitting next to her. Except for a tightening around his mouth, he showed no outward reaction to the new arrival. He nodded in greeting as Eric took the seat Iris offered him. When the conversation resumed, they avoided talking to each other beyond a few civilities.

Jessica never got the chance to answer the question Peter had asked her or to find out where it had been leading. In time she said, "Iris, why don't we begin dinner? Eric, you'll stay, won't you?" She turned to Peter. "Mr. Savage, would you care to join us?"

He gave her an unreadable look before rising to his feet.

"No, thank you, Mrs. Romney. I have a date for dinner." With a rather abrupt farewell all around, he left.

Jessica found herself strangely smarting from the rebuff.

chapter 8

RETURNING TO ROMNEY HOUSE three months after she had taken her last, sorrowful look at it was something Jessica had dreaded. It would be like seeing a lover in someone else's arms, she had imagined. And she had loved the place, as much as a house can be loved, from the first day it had become her home. But she had told Peter Savage that returning to it would not bother her. Now she had to prove it to him and herself.

The moment she drove through the tall massive iron gates, still bearing the ornately wrought "R," the changes Peter had made in even so brief a time became obvious. That air of shabbiness, of having seen better times, was gone. The house and its surrounding grounds were now as richly tended, as grand and imposing as they had been in the days when it had been the most magnificent property for many miles around.

Romney House had been built along the classically severe lines of the Georgian style. It was a large, gracefully proportioned building constructed of the local honey-colored sandstone, with a wide, many-columned veranda that embraced it on three sides. In the same hospitable tradition that was characteristic of many of America's Southern mansions, the veranda on either side led to "strangers' rooms"—accommodation for late-night visitors who could make themselves at home without disturbing the household.

All around the veranda were shuttered French doors

leading to the cool depths of the large, high-ceilinged rooms. A fanlighted front door, again bearing an ornate "R," opened into a cavernous hall from which a central staircase led to the upper floor.

The house had been built in the early part of the nineteenth century, when more than eight hundred acres of rich farmland had been granted to a Romney ancestor by the governor of New South Wales. Since then the land had dwindled to less than a hundred acres, a small portion of which Jessica had been able to retain and was now leasing out. The rest had been sold with the house to the new owner.

Jessica eased her car along the freshly graveled drive, and saw that the house had not so much undergone renovation as skillful and faithful restoration. A portion of the roof was newly tiled with material that matched the original Welsh slate tiles. The upstairs windows, whose frames and sashes had been so badly decayed that it had been dangerous to open them, had been replaced by replicas of the old ones. The veranda was newly flagged with old stones that appeared to have been there for a hundred years. One of the columns that had badly needed propping up had been either replaced or repaired so skillfully that she couldn't tell which had been done. Somehow Peter had managed to renew and refresh the place without intruding on the dignity of its age.

To Jessica's surprise and relief, her reunion with the much loved house was more pleasant than she had expected. When she had first come to it, it had already fallen into a somewhat neglected state. She was reassured to see that it was now as cared for as it deserved to be.

She parked the car under the shade of a giant gum tree and walked toward it. So many memories tied her to the house. Its loss could still stir her pain. As she stood gazing up at the building before her, Peter Savage rounded the corner and, spotting her, hurried over.

"It looks beautiful. You've performed a miracle," she complimented him by way of greeting.

He looked at her carefully, as if trying to measure her

true feelings behind the polite words.

"How did you manage all this in such a short time?" she asked.

"It helps to be in the business," he replied. "I hired a large crew and kept at them with a whip. And I did some of the work myself." His questioning look was still on her. "Do you really approve?" he asked.

"Everything is exactly as it should be," she said.

His eyes followed hers, and for a while they stood together looking at the house. "I haven't really changed anything," he said, turning to her. There was an odd note in his voice, as if he were trying to reassure her.

"I can see that," she agreed. "But there is one thing you *should* change," she suggested, and when he looked at her questioningly, she went on, "You should remove that 'R' from above the entrance. And from the gate."

He shook his head. "The 'R' stays. It's still Romney House and will remain that while I have it."

She threw him a quick, surprised glance. He had almost sounded as if he meant the words as some sort of offering. "Don't you have any dynastic ambitions?" she chided to cover her confusion. "Oh, I forgot, you're off marriage for life, right?"

He paused for just an instant before agreeing. "Right." Which left an awkward silence between them. Jessica, anxious to channel the conversation in a different direction, said briskly, "Well, I'd better get on with the business that brought me."

"Would you like to see the inside first?" he invited.

"No." Jessica shook her head, drawing another measuring look from him. The visit was not nearly as painful as she had feared, but she didn't feel ready yet to be shown through the home that, in her heart at least, she felt was still hers. "We have a great deal to do," she added.

They went to the small building where the outdoor furniture was stored, and with the help of two workmen they sorted and stacked the tables, benches, and folding chairs that would be used for the fete in two days.

When they were finished they strolled about the grounds deciding where booths, tents, and tables should be set up and how to best protect the flower beds from the crowds. She glanced at him questioningly each time she made a suggestion, but he insisted on leaving all the decisions to her, so that for a while she almost felt as if she were the mistress of the house again.

When the time came to show Peter the dishes, glasses, and cutlery that would have to be unpacked for the occasion, she could no longer avoid going inside the house. They entered through a back vestibule that led into a passage with a scullery on one side and a vast kitchen on the other.

Once the kitchen had been a rather dingy place where meals were prepared and where Jessica conferred once a day with the housekeeper about menus. It had not been a place she had ever cared to linger in, but a wonderful transformation had made it into a cozy, homey room that looked comfortable and inviting.

Everything that had been broken or shabby had been fixed or replaced without giving the room a too new, sterile look. An enormous old fuel stove that had not been used for many years had been made efficient with newly fitted gas pipes. The cavernous fireplace that had been boarded up had been opened again, ready to warm the room on winter days. A refrigerator and freezer were concealed in pantries on either side of the kitchen, and the flooring had been stripped to its original foundation of slate slabs worn smooth and polished with age. Built-in cupboards had been ripped out in most of the kitchen and replaced by old-fashioned oak and pine dressers, and in the center of the room stood a large pine table.

That Peter's expertise had run to constructing an authentic-looking Victorian kitchen was amazing, but Jessica thought the room's size and function a little absurd for a lone bachelor. Perhaps he planned to do a lot of entertaining. Her fascination with this delightful room made her forget her reluctance to see the inside of the house, and only when they had unpacked the china, glasses, and cutlery did she accept his renewed offer to show her around.

She went with him through the familiar rooms in the alien role of visitor. It was a strange feeling, but the apprehension and sadness she felt at the beginning of the tour began to lessen as she took in with satisfaction and pleasure everything around her. As with the outside, Peter had made as few changes as possible.

Curtains, upholstery, wallpaper, and rugs all appeared strangely familiar, until Jessica realized that they were close copies of the originals. Peter must have gone to some trouble in his research.

In every room on the ground floor the improvements were evident. The library—a favorite room of the Romneys—had a newly laid floor that replaced the original, which had been warped by rain leaking from the roof. The drawing rooms had been repainted and repapered. In the small conservatory the glass-domed ceiling had been repaired, and in the dining hall the marble fireplace mantel, cracked for many years, had been replaced by a perfect replica. Jessica felt as if she was glancing back into the past and seeing the house as if she had never known it.

She examined Peter's collection of eighteenth-century English furniture with special admiration, deciding she preferred it to the ornate and fussy Victorian pieces with which the house originally had been filled.

Many things had surprised her about Peter Savage before, but nothing so much as seeing his house. It wasn't the house of a newly rich man who had hastily collected about him as many acquisitions as possible. It looked like the home of someone who knew exactly what he wanted and who settled for nothing less. Was this the same man she had first met in faded work clothes by the side of the road? The same man who had taken her to the most run-down place he could find for their first date? Their *only* date, she reminded herself.

He did not invite her upstairs, not, she suspected, because he was bashful about showing her his bedrooms but because he sensed that that part of the house still held too many painful associations for her.

When the tour ended and they returned to the hall, she complimented him on everything, but secretly she felt that something was lacking. Everything was perfect, all beautifully done, yet the house felt incomplete, as if it were waiting for something.

Uncannily Peter echoed her thoughts. "A little lifeless, don't you agree?" he asked.

Startled, she considered the question. "It needs ... people. It's far too big for a man alone."

"So women like to point out to me," he said dryly.

She frowned. Do they indeed? she thought indignantly. Being lumped together with other women like that was not very flattering, worse, but his implication was downright insulting. She imagined there were plenty of women who would hint and offer themselves as desirable companions, but did the insufferable, conceited man think that was what *she* was doing? Too bad he hasn't asked one of the others to help him out, she thought savagely.

She gave him a frosty glance and realized her thoughts must have shown on her face, for he seemed greatly amused by what he read there. And only a moment before she had been admiring him!

"I think just about everything is ready. The rest can't be done until the morning of the fete," Jessica told him briskly, unable to keep a slight chill out of her voice.

"Thank you," he said, amusement evident in his voice.

Looking past him, Jessica added tonelessly, "Not at all. Now that you know how it's done, you'll be able to handle it on your own next time."

"I'm thanking you for more than that." Something in his voice compelled her to look at him. He had moved so close that if she had turned a fraction she would have brushed against him. "I'm thanking you for coming over here at last. I know it wasn't easy for you." His face was serious as he spoke.

"Nonsense, you make too much of that," she said,

looking away. "Anyway, I'm glad I saw the place.... It has never looked lovelier." The admission cost her some small effort.

He seemed to realize it, for his voice held an uncharacteristic gentleness. "Then that's all that matters." It was such a strange thing to hear from a man who never sought approval that she looked up at him. But as their eyes met, something guarded stole over his face, and in a moment his voice was full of irony again.

"It's a relief, anyway. For a while I thought we'd remain feuding neighbors forever. Like those countrymen of yours—what were their names... the Hatfields and the McCoys?"

"Oh, I wouldn't light the peace pipes yet, Mr. Savage," she warned him with equal flippancy.

On the brief drive home she meditated over the set pattern of their encounters. No matter how they began or how they progressed, they always ended in inevitable friction. She couldn't remember a single time that they had parted on a friendly note.

The annual Sommerville Fete was always a popular event, but on this hot summer morning a record number of people had turned up for it. There were the regulars who always attended, and there were the curious who had come from far and wide to see how Romney House was faring under its new owner—and to take a look at the new owner himself. Even before midmorning, the members of the ladies' committee who were responsible for organizing the event were rubbing their hands with glee at the sum of money they had collected in entrance fees. This plus the proceeds from the sales of the various stalls would be divided between the small district hospital, the local old people's home, and a scholarship fund for a local agricultural college.

The grounds of Romney House looked gay and festive. Tents, awnings, and stalls had been set up at dawn and now displayed an irresistible array of homemade goods—fruit pies and tarts, twenty different varieties of cakes, small pastries, scones with strawberry jam and fresh whipped cream, potbellied jars of homegrown preserves and honey, savory sausage rolls and meat patties, pickles and jams, toffees and fudge. Other stalls sold the handiwork of local women—crocheted, knitted, or embroidered, hand-painted or modeled.

One section of the garden had been roped off for the flower show, where blooms of every scent and hue vied in brilliant competition.

Children, stuffing themselves with unaccustomed allowances of cakes and candies, ran riot, while their busy parents indulged themselves in a frenzy of buying. By mid morning it looked as if every item in every stall would be sold.

Jessica, crisp and cool in a pale pink cotton dress and white sandals, went from stall to stall, helping wherever she was needed. Supervising the cashboxes was one of her responsibilities. She had seen little of Peter Savage, having exchanged only a few words with him early that morning when she and several other women had arrived to help set things up. But she caught sight of him now and then, always surrounded by a crowd, usually a crowd of women. For a man who claimed to be unaccustomed to entertaining, he seemed perfectly at ease.

Iris, wearing an enormous picture hat and an extravagantly flounced lilac chiffon dress, came over to where Jessica was piling neat stacks of coins in one of the booths. Iris had been unusually subdued when they'd arrived that morning, this being her first return to her old home. But the instant sale of her Black Forest cakes, her towering, rich Pavlovas, and her other exotic contributions to the fete had cheered her up, and now she was in a gay mood.

"What a crush! Have you ever seen such a crowd?" she asked, fanning herself. "The last time such a number turned up was when they all came to have a look at you." For a moment both women's eyes grew sad with memories. They exchanged rueful smiles, then Jessica said cheerfully, "The money's simply rolling in. It's going

Beyond Pride

to make a great start for that new hospital wing."

"Well, I didn't think I would, but I'm quite enjoying myself," Iris declared. "I'm sorry we couldn't persuade Mother to come."

"I think it was a little too much to ask of her."

"I suppose so," Iris conceded. "At least she was spared some of the comments I received. You know, the type that goes 'My dear, how awful it must be for you to come back here as a visitor.' Well-meaning people can be so tactless." Jessica had been subjected to similar remarks that morning and now looked sympathetically at Iris, who gave her a quick smile. "Never mind. Keeping one's chin up does wonders for a sagging neck." The two women laughed.

At that moment Peter Savage appeared at the booth. Taking in their smiling faces, he declared, "Whatever you women are selling, I'll take all you've got."

Iris gave him an impertinent smile. "You're the one who should be selling."

"Me? What?" he asked in surprise.

"Judging from the crowd of women around you all morning, you'd be a bigger riot than a fire sale if you opened a kissing booth—with you behind the counter, of course. The proceeds from that alone would be enough to build a whole new hospital."

He pretended to think the proposition over. "Anything for charity. If I did, would you be buying?"

"Not me," Jessica declared with spirit, slamming down the lid of a cashbox. "I always did hate standing in line." Giving him a level look, she picked up the box and left the booth.

"Come early and avoid the rush," he called after her with a mocking laugh.

Toward late morning the crowd's energy began to flag. Too much food, too much to drink, too much rushing about in the heat had taken its toll. People sought refuge on benches under the shade of the giant gum trees or on rugs spread out on the grass. The very young and the very old took naps, while those in between fanned themselves exhaustedly and listened to a local band that substituted noisy enthusiasm for harmony.

Everyone was resting up for the main event, the barbecue Peter Savage had offered to throw in the afternoon to boost attendance.

Jessica and Marjorie Cunningham sipped cups of tea while conferring over the day's takings.

"It's such a success," Marjorie rejoiced, looking at the impressive figures. "I must say I'm quite surprised by how obliging Mr. Savage has been about the whole thing. You know, I was reluctant to ask him at first. There's something well...cynical about him. In the beginning I really didn't think he was our kind."

"And you do now?" Jessica asked, annoyed at the woman's snobbery.

"Oh yes, I think he's quite a gentleman."

Jessica thought with irony of Peter's opinion of Marjorie's beloved Lilac Ball and suppressed a smile. "And what elevated him to that status in your esteem?" she inquired.

"Well, he couldn't have been nicer when I put the thing to him. He was willing to do anything to—" Suddenly Marjorie stopped and whispered in Jessica's ear. "Don't look now, dear, but there's a very strange-looking man staring at us."

This was enough to make Jessica look up at once. A vaguely familiar man came toward them. He was dressed in a riotously patterned floral shirt, opened low enough to reveal the splendor of a large tattoo. His hands were thrust into the pockets of a pair of baggy and shiny checked pants, and on his head he wore an old army slouch hat at a rakish angle.

"Charlie," Jessica exclaimed, recognizing the publican of the Royal Victoria. "How nice to see you here."

"Hello, love," he said, taking the hand she had extended. "Just thought I'd look in on the doings. Pete invited me and the boys," he explained, jerking a thumb over his shoulder to indicate a group of men who looked bashfully in their direction. Jessica recognized some of

Beyond Pride 105

the faces as belonging to patrons of Charlie's hotel.

"Well, that *is* nice," she said warmly. "I'm very glad you came."

During this exchange Marjorie had stood by, her eyes fairly popping out of her head as she stared at the festively attired Charlie. Becoming aware of her scrutiny, he turned his own frank gaze on her and stared back measure for measure. Marjorie, unaccustomed to male attention of any sort, seemed undecided between looking huffed or flattered.

Jessica introduced them. "Marjorie, I'd like you to meet a friend of Mr. Savage—and mine. Charlie Travis, Miss Marjorie Cunningham. Mr. Travis owns the Royal Victoria. You know, that picturesque little place out by the railway lines."

Marjorie sniffed. "I don't believe I've ever heard of it."

"You ought to come 'round one night, love. Give you a free beer," Charlie said, adding this seemingly irresistible offer to his invitation. The expression on Marjorie's face was wonderful to behold, but Charlie was not rebuffed. He appeared to find something fascinating in her despite her haughty demeanor. In the background the amateur band launched into a lively dance number, drawing some hardy souls onto a makeshift floor that had been erected for the purpose.

"Care to dance?" he asked her.

Marjorie drew back, flustered. "I'm afraid I'm far too busy, Mr.—er—Travis," she muttered, fussing with some already neatly folded tablecloths.

"Call me Charlie," he suggested informally and went on to press his suit. "It's a shame to keep a good-looking girl like you out of circulation all day." Marjorie, who had not been called a girl for the better part of thirty years, and never in her memory a good-looking one, blushed violently.

Jessica observed these developments with great enjoyment. She cut in to back up Charlie. "Absolutely right, Marjorie. You've been working too hard all morning. It's time you took a break."

"Tell you what;" Charlie said as if to clinch the argument. "See this fiver?" he asked, pulling a five-dollar note from his pocket. "I'll donate it to your charity just to show you I'm not wasting your time."

"Really, Mr. Travis!" Marjorie exclaimed with indignation that didn't quite hide the fact that she was flattered. After all, Charlie was a handsome, robust-looking man.

"But Marjorie," Jessica protested in a loud whisper, "we need every penny we can get. It *is* for charity."

That did it. Marjorie drew herself up, ready to do her all. "Very well, Mr. Travis. I shall have one dance with you."

With a sly, triumphant wink at Jessica, he took Marjorie by the arm and led her onto the platform that had been set up for dancing.

Jessica watched them with delight. What perfect timing, she thought with glee, recalling Marjorie's allusions to "our kind" a few minutes before. As she stood, fascinated, Peter Savage, hands in his pockets, ambled over and leaned against a corner of the booth.

"Am I hallucinating in the heat, or can I believe my eyes?" he asked, watching the couple with interest.

"You can believe them," Jessica assured him.

"You look rather pleased about it," he observed. "Did you have anything to do with it?"

"Not a thing. It was something—I'm not sure what— at first sight."

He shook his head in disbelief. "If for nothing else, the fete was worth holding just to see that. I know they'll get on. They have so much in common." When Jessica looked at him questioningly, he explained, "She puts great store by her convict ancestry, and I happen to know for a fact that Charlie spent half his time in the brig during his wild years in the navy."

"What's all the chuckling about?" Iris demanded, joining them.

Jessica pointed toward Marjorie and her new beau and explained briefly, leaving out the details of her own first acquaintance with Charlie. Iris joined in their laughter. They chatted about the morning's events for a while, then Iris said, "I haven't had a chance to congratulate you yet, Mr. Savage, on the wonders you've done with the place." He thanked her, and she added, looking at him curiously, "Jessie tells me you plan to keep Romney House as its name."

"That's right," he confirmed. "Buckingham Palace hasn't been renamed just because the Duke of Buckingham no longer lives there, has it?" He smiled.

"Oh, Carlotta will love the analogy when I tell her that," Iris cried in delight.

Peter turned to Jessica. "If Charlie succeeded, maybe I can too. Will you dance?"

"I have rather a lot to do," Jessica replied evasively, hearing herself almost echo Marjorie's words. She hoped she didn't sound quite as unconvincing as Marjorie had.

"I'll take over for you," Iris offered at once. Jessica looked hesitantly toward the dance floor, equally divided between wanting to dance with him and wanting to avoid all contact with him as much as possible.

"Don't fall all over yourself with unbridled enthusiasm," he said sarcastically, taking one of her elbows. As she was about to decide in favor of dancing, a pretty young blonde, whom Jessica had observed hovering about him all morning, came up and took his arm possessively.

"You promised to have a couple of dances with me," she wheedled. "Remember?"

Jessica drew back at once. He looked at her for a moment, but she turned her back to him and busied herself at the booth.

"How could I forget?" she heard him say with flattering gallantry. When she turned around a few moments later they were already closely entwined on the dance floor. Iris gave her a disapproving shake of her head, but said nothing.

The barbecue began in the early afternoon. Mounds of thick steaks, chops, and sausages were wheeled out on kitchen carts next to two giant barbecues standing back to back. Hundreds of potatoes, wrapped in silver foil, had been already baking in the ashes for more than an hour. The air was filled with the savory aroma of frying onions and sizzling meat. Ears of corn stood cooking in two enormous caldrons, and on serving tables stood tubs of salads and coleslaw. Half a dozen barrels of draft beer were on tap, and dozens of bottles of wine made from grapes, grown in South Australia's vineyards, were cooling in mountains of ice.

Everyone's energy and appetite revived again, and tables and chairs were set up by eager hands. The grounds of Romney House rang with laughter, music, and children's shrieks.

Jessica, Iris, and Eric, who had only just arrived, took their places at one of the smaller tables under the trees, where they were soon joined by Marjorie and Charlie. Marjorie looked half embarrassed, half pleased. She usually sat with other unattached women, always the organizer, never the participant at these events. Now a flatteringly attentive man sat at her side who solicitously attended to her every need, fetching food and drink for her.

Jessica had not talked with Peter Savage again since his offer of a dance three hours before. He had stayed on the dance floor for a long time with a succession of pretty partners, and later he had been busy organizing the barbecue. Now he was propped up on an elbow on a blanket in the shade, surrounded by a half-dozen young women.

A feeling of wrenching loneliness swept over Jessica. Everyone seemed to be coupled off, even Marjorie and Iris, who seemed to have a growing new understanding with Eric.

Her loneliness was not lessened by her presence in the garden of the house where she had known such happiness. Resolutely she kept her eyes from the spot where Peter Savage sat among his harem.

When the meal was finished, she decided to go off

quietly by herself. She had worked hard since early morning, and her head was beginning to buzz, heralding the beginnings of a headache. It was too hot, too boisterous, with too many people around. She wished she could go home, but she had to stay until the end to count the final proceeds for the day.

She stole away unobserved and took a path through the neatly trimmed shrubbery that she knew led to a quiet, remote section of the garden. Rounding the corner of the small summerhouse, she heard her name called softly, and, startled, she turned around.

He was standing in the too low doorway of the building.

"What are you doing here?" she asked, recognizing at once the absurdity of the question. It was his house, after all.

"Counting myself down and out," he replied, running a hand wearily over his face. "I've had all I can take of this squire of the manor bit!"

"Really? It looked like you were enjoying every moment of it."

He understood her meaning at once and gave her an insufferable, knowing look. "Jealous?" he teased, coming down the steps to peer at her closely. "No, I can see not. Well, don't let my remarkable performance fool you. I wish they'd all go home."

Glancing at him, Jessica saw that he was genuinely tired. He had not stopped playing the courteous, attentive host all day. "I'm afraid they won't go home for quite a while yet," she told him.

"Then let's go into hiding. Can I walk with you?"

She shrugged. "I can't very well stop you. It *is* your home," she pointed out.

"That's right," he snorted. "Take my breath away with your graciousness." Jessica reflected on the invariable abrasiveness of their conversations. For her part, it served as a mantle of protection against an undefined threat she always felt in his company. But he came to her side and, adjusting his steps to hers, walked with her in silence.

She led the way to a far corner of the garden and stopped at a small arbor covered with a rich growth of jasmine and climbing roses. This shady bower had always been her favorite spot, and she had brought him here without thinking.

Jessica sat on a wooden bench shaded by the arbor while Peter sat in the grass at her feet, leaning his back against the bench, one arm propped on it for support, his long legs drawn under him. From here the noise of the fete was a distant hum, drowned out by a multitude of bees attracted by the rich, sweet fragrance of the flowers.

The serenity of the moment took Jessica's breath away. She thought of the hours she had spent here in solitude, reading and listening to music. Incredibly, telepathically, the thought communicated itself to him.

"This is your favorite place," he said, not as a question but as a fact.

He turned around for confirmation and caught a look in her eyes that she had been unable to hide. With a single urgent movement he was on the bench beside her, taking off the small straw hat she had put on for her walk, his fingers sliding through her loose hair. His movements became lingering, unhurried, as if he knew she was powerless to move, helpless to resist. Slowly, taking pleasure in delaying the inevitable, he stroked her hair, traced the outlines of her face, and slid his hands lightly down her arms to take her hands in his. He leaned closer to inhale the fragrance of her hair, then, bringing his mouth within a fraction of her own, he waited, forcing her to respond. She closed her eyes and, with a gasp at her shattered restraint, swayed forward, her lips parting. A tremor passed through her in the instant of contact, but he pulled her so fiercely close that in a moment it was stilled.

His lips brushed gently across hers, teasing her, then probed deeper, tasting the sweetness of her mouth. Slowly his touch grew more demanding until after a breathless, oblivious eternity, he drew away with a movement that seemed to cost him great effort. She looked into his eyes, shadowed with the intensity of passion, and saw that he had only drawn away for the pleasure of kissing her again. A vein was hammering in his neck, and she heard his barely controlled breathing and knew he was in her power as much as she was in his.

"Oh, hell," he swore hoarsely in a surrender she thought more passionate, more complete, than any love words could have been.

Even the small distance between them became unendurable, and they swayed toward each other again, her hands flying up to pull him closer to her. His response was almost violent. His rasping breath became mingled with her shallow, quickened breaths. Their kiss opened a floodgate of desire, its torrent overwhelming her. His hand left her waist to press against her breast, and her own flew up defensively, only to fall helplessly away again. The bruising hardness of his teeth, the scorching imprint of the hand raised to her breast, filled her with unthinkable urgencies. Unthinkable! a dim, still conscious part of her brain warned. The warning grew from a small, feeble protest into a self-protective panic that finally gave her the strength to pull away.

"No!" she whispered, the flush of desire draining away to leave her face pale. "No!" she repeated in a louder but not yet steady voice. "I don't want this!"

He looked at her, his face and voice still reflecting the passion that had consumed them a moment ago. "You can say that to me when all I have to do is reach out to feel your pulse racing?" he asked huskily, his eyes so demanding that she had to look away. She tried to move from his embrace, but his hands restrained her. He reached under her chin, lifting her head to look at him again, and this time his voice took on a harder edge as his hand bit into her arm.

"We're back to that again, I see." His strong mouth drew down at the corners. "If it was me you were fighting, I'd know how to go about winning. But you're fighting yourself. It's a pretense. Give it up." He tried to pull her to him, but she wrenched away.

Give it up! he told her with that detestable self-assurance, speaking like a man used to unconditional surrender. A forbidding coldness forced itself into Jessica's eyes, and a sense of combat flared inside her.

"Let go of me now, please," she commanded in an icily calm voice. His arrogance had helped her to win back her self-control. His assurance that her conquest was as inevitable as his conquest of every other woman that day allowed her to think clearly again. "The only thing I'm fighting is a touch of self-disgust!" she told him with contempt.

He drew a deep breath, and for a moment she saw a menacing expression pass across his face. "What is it that disgusts you about yourself, Jessica? Those rare moments of honesty you can't help giving into?" he demanded harshly.

"Honesty?" she flared bitterly. "What's honest about... kissing a man you don't like?" There, she had come out and told him at last.

But he didn't flinch at her words. "To hell with *liking* me," he countered fiercely. "Leave that sentiment to Eric Cuttler. I want you—and you want me!"

Despite her bitterness, the words spoken so frankly and with such conviction freshly aroused unwanted emotions in her. To escape them, she jumped from the seat and, white-faced, her eyes darkening to a stormy green, she turned on him. "I think you and I have said far too much to each other already and need say no more. Ever!"

"Except for one more thing," he responded with a sneer, barring her path. "The next time you pull one of your little displays of affection for Cuttler, we'll both know what a bloody farce it is."

chapter 9

BY THE TIME Iris and Carlotta were up the next morning, Jessica had packed a small overnight bag and announced she was going to Sydney on the afternoon train on a matter of business that had suddenly come up.

During a mostly sleepless night she had decided she had to get away, if only for a brief time. She knew running off would accomplish nothing in the long run, but for the moment that didn't matter. She didn't look beyond the relief of a day or two of solitude.

Fortunately Iris and Carlotta were not hard to convince of the urgency of the trip. On the matter of business they left everything to Jessica unquestioningly. And she did have some business to transact in Sydney, she told herself, to add weight to her decision to leave, though not of a nature her in-laws could have known. In the overnight case were carefully wrapped pieces of her jewelry, which she wanted to sell in the city. Taxes and insurance on the house were due soon, and some costly repairs to the plumbing could no longer be put off. The amounts involved would be too much of a strain on her present budget, and rather than touch their tiny capital, which Eric was advising her to reinvest, she would raise the money this way.

It was still bright daylight, though almost seven o'clock at night, when she arrived at the vast bustling Central Railway Station in downtown Sydney. Outside she joined an orderly line at a taxi stand and gave the driver the address of a small private hotel in Castlereagh Street. It was an old-fashioned, quiet hotel frequented mostly by country visitors and central to everything, but not nearly as costly as the great modern city hotels. Gone were the days when the Romneys had a large suite reserved for them at the most luxurious hotel.

Though she went to Sydney often, Jessica never ceased to be amazed at how Australia's largest city continually changed and expanded before her eyes. Day by day it was growing at breakneck speed into the most important and cosmopolitan metropolis in the southern part of the world.

Jessica's hotel was in the quiet, downtown section of the city, which had changed little. The other buildings were smaller, private businesses, and—perfect for her purposes—antique jewelers and auction houses.

Jessica had used the hotel several times in recent months and was greeted with friendly recognition by the woman behind the reception desk. She registered, took her key, and carried her bag to the ancient, creaking elevator.

She unpacked quickly in the small, airless room with its narrow twin beds, scarred dressing table, and rickety wardrobe. After hanging up the two dresses she had brought, she sprinkled bath salts in the tub, and turned on the taps full force. The water came up in shuddering fits and starts through the ancient plumbing. While the tub was filling, she unpacked the two small boxes in which she had put her jewelry.

Three items were of particular value—a magnificent jade bangle, a pair of matching long drop earrings, and a tiny pendant watch, its case encrusted with precious stones. Jessica held the pieces lovingly in her hands, remembering the birthday and anniversary on which her husband had given them to her. They were precious to her, but not as precious as the mother and sister he had left in her care. With a determined movement she pushed the jewels away.

Only when she was soaking in the warm, scented bath

did she finally allow her mind to turn to what had driven her to Sydney in such haste. She could no longer pretend it did not exist; she had to recognize it, face it head on, and, most important, fight it.

But she couldn't even name what it was. Was it desire? Passion? Something as obscene as lust? Though she shrank from the words, she used them ruthlessly against herself, because she knew no others to describe the way she felt about Peter Savage.

Certainly it wasn't love. Her feelings for Peter Savage were so far removed from anything she had ever felt for a man, so completely different from what she had felt for Roderick, it could not be love. Then how could it be so powerful that it occupied all her waking thoughts and filled her with helplessness, even fear? She sank deeper into the fragrant water as if trying to hide from the shameful questions.

Peter Savage had never spoken a single, endearing word to her. Instead, he had boldly told her "I want you." Remembering his words made her shiver. No one had ever said that to her without first prefacing it with a declaration of love. She had always flattered herself on being hardheaded and sensible, but was she in fact, terribly naive? At twenty-seven, had she already passed beyond the right to expect something more than just a physical bond? Was this the course a modern, mature relationship took? If it was, she wanted no part of it. But no, she told herself the next instant, it wasn't the way of the world, just the way of Peter Savage.

Her nerves were stretched so tautly with these thoughts that when the telephone rang she jumped, splashing bathwater over the side of the tub. Stepping out of the bath and hastily wrapping a towel around herself, she went to answer it.

"Hello?" she asked apprehensively.

"Jessica, it's Eric."

Relief flooded her as she greeted him. He was calling, he explained, because he had just spoken with Iris and learned she was in town. He suggested they have dinner, during which he would be able to give her a briefing about the investments he proposed to make on her behalf.

"Oh Eric, I'd love to, but honestly I'm completely exhausted. I was just taking a bath, after which I planned to fall into bed."

"What about lunch tomorrow, then?"

"I have some business to take care of in the morning, and I don't know if I'll be finished in time," she said, glancing at the two small jewel boxes beside the phone. "But I won't be returning to Sommerville until the day after—how about lunch then?" she proposed. Eric agreed, and she hung up.

Jessica toweled herself absently while her thoughts returned to Peter Savage. Distance hadn't lent clarity to her thoughts. They were in as much turmoil as ever.

Savage's contradictory character confused her. She remembered his generosity, his offers of help, his concern, his sudden, unexpected switches to gentleness. Then she remembered his harsh, arrogant words.

Restlessly she moved to the open window and looked at the lamp-lit street below her. How her decision to remain in Sommerville had turned against her, she thought bitterly. She had known it wouldn't be easy living in the shadow of Romney House, but she hadn't anticipated this kind of conflict with its new owner. And now she was trapped. It was too late to move, and her pride, now more than ever, held her there. He had been right in a way. She wasn't fighting him as much as herself.

She reached for the nightgown she had laid out on one of the beds, then put it back. She was too agitated, too restless to go to bed yet. She would take a stroll around the streets, perhaps have dinner, maybe even go to a movie. She had come to Sydney to think things out, but there was only so much thinking one could do before one's mind became too benumbed to function, she decided.

She put on fresh underwear and took the simpler of the two dresses she had brought, a gray-mauve silk shift with small slits in the skirt. She was just zipping up her dress when the phone rang again.

Frowning, Jessica answered it. "Mrs. Romney? A gentleman down here to see you," the woman at the reception desk announced. Eric must have decided to come over after all. She knew his office wasn't far away. Well, since he had come, she would go down and see him, she decided with an exasperated sigh.

"Please have him wait, I'll be down at once," she told the receptionist with resignation.

"Damn!" she muttered, making hasty adjustments to her hair. She had come all this way to be alone and now... Instantly contrite, she adjusted her face into a more welcoming expression.

But when the elevator door creaked open on the ground floor and she stepped into the lobby, her smile of anticipation swiftly changed to an incredulous stare. Peter Savage extricated himself from the depths of an armchair that was too small for him and came toward her. He studied her for a moment before his mouth formed the familiar sardonic smile.

"Restrain yourself, please," he addressed her. "Your wildly emotional greeting is drawing a crowd."

"What are you doing here?" Jessica demanded, continuing to stare in disbelief.

"Expecting someone else?" he asked, taking in her freshly dressed, combed, and perfumed appearance.

"Not you!" she retorted. "How did you find me? How did you get to Sydney?"

"I called at your place this afternoon, and your sister-in-law told me where you were. I flew here in a chopper—got to Sydney before you, as a matter of fact—and was on my way to pick you up from the station, but I was held up in traffic from the heliport."

The information whirled about in Jessica's brain. He had called at her house, followed her to Sydney, and now he was standing in front of her as composed as if yesterday hadn't happened.

"Now you answer my question," he ordered. "Were

you expecting someone else?"

"Never mind that!" Jessica snapped, beginning to recover. "What do you want?"

He laughed at her. "To take you out to dinner."

She looked at him suspiciously. "You came all this way to go out to dinner?"

"I'd fly to China to take you to dinner." He bowed with exaggerated gallantry, while a hint of secret amusement lurked in his eyes.

"You'd be wasting your time on a futile trip, as you have just now. I'm on my way to bed," she informed him.

"Really?" he asked, giving her another significant once-over.

Jessica knew her freshly groomed appearance belied her words, but she didn't care. She didn't owe this man any explanations.

"Really," she replied coolly.

"Well, good night, then," he said with apparent resignation, sitting down in the armchair again. He slid deeply into it, stretching his legs out before him, and made a show of settling in for a long time.

"What are you doing?" Jessica demanded, regarding him warily.

"Making myself comfortable for the night," he told her pleasantly. "I want to make sure I'm here on time to take you to breakfast in the morning."

Jessica looked about the lobby uneasily. With most men this threat would be sheer bluff. With Peter Savage, she couldn't be sure.

"You're not used to taking no for an answer, are you?" she accused him, trying hard to keep a grip on her composure.

"I should be from you, because that's the only answer I ever get, but you're right. It's not something I'd like to get used to." The determination in his voice was unmistakable.

Jessica glanced about once more. Half a dozen elderly visitors stood about the lobby, all speaking in genteel,

Beyond Pride

subdued whispers. However she was going to deal with this, it had better not be here. Damn him, he had trapped her again!

"I'll have to go upstairs to change." Her voice was steady, but her glance at him was murderous.

His face softened at once as he leaped out of his chair. "No, don't," he said. "You look perfect just as you are."

Jessica gave him a pert look. "Are you sure? I thought I'd slip into something more suitable for where you're bound to take me—like jeans and a leather jacket."

He grinned in understanding. "No dives tonight. We'll go wherever you want."

She gave him a last skeptical glance before stepping into the elevator. In her room she opened the wardrobe, then shut it. No, she wouldn't change into her more formal dress; the evening wouldn't last long enough to make it worthwhile. She slammed drawers as she gathered her makeup and threw it into her purse. The everlasting nerve of the man! She had come all this way to get away from him, and he had the gall to turn up right in the middle of Sydney and once more force her to do something she didn't want to do.

Why was he doing it? she asked her reflection in the mirror. Why this elaborate pursuit? Perhaps she was the only woman who had ever said no to him, and he considered her a challenge. And while she was still smarting from their awful clash the day before, he appeared to have already forgotten it.

As she stood in front of the mirror, she saw that her hands weren't quite steady. She tried to blame her anger, but she knew deep down that something more disturbing was responsible. A small flare of excitement was beginning to mingle with her resentment.

Peter had a small sports car waiting outside the hotel. "I keep it parked at the heliport," he explained. "But if you're afraid of being blown about, we could get a cab."

"No, I like open cars. I used to have one like this myself," she replied, adding with a sideways glance at him, "As long as the seat belt works properly."

He gave her a slow, impertinent smile. "Haven't had time to tinker with this one yet."

Jessica had decided to make the evening as short as possible, but now, as he asked her where she wanted to eat, she hesitated. It was an oppressively hot evening after a scorching day. She thought of her hot, stuffy room at the hotel, then of the ocean breezes and the pleasure of driving in an open car. Her resolution weakened as he proposed a restaurant by the sea, and she accepted.

He headed the car east, out of the inner city's narrow streets. They drove past the green expanse of Hyde Park, up traffic-choked William Street, through King's Cross—Sydney's down-at-the-heel version of Broadway—and through Soho, the district that came alive as the sun went down.

Once they left this bottleneck of traffic, the road became more open through the old wealthy suburb of Woollahra with its immaculately renovated rows of Victorian terrace houses, through the exclusive districts around Rose Bay with their mansions and luxury apartment buildings commanding some of the most breathtaking views of Sydney Harbour, out to Watson's Bay, the easternmost tip of the city.

They parked the car before a restaurant that had been built on a pier jutting into the bay. They were led to a table by one of the windows with a panoramic view of the darkening water.

Jessica, who had sampled the best seafood from New Orleans to New England, thought the Australian variety was the best in the world. The small local rock oysters were the most flavorsome she had ever tasted, and the huge lobsters and prawns were incomparably sweet and succulent.

She chose a cold seafood platter with salad, and Peter ordered a John Dory fish and selected a light white wine from South Australia. After the waiter had taken their orders, Jessica sat looking out into the darkness, pinpricked with the lights of distant houses on the opposite shore. Here and there she could see the dim outline of a moored boat bobbing up and down in peaceful rhythm on the black water. A fat candle flickered on the table between them, fanned by a warm breeze off the bay.

After a while Jessica became conscious of Peter's eyes on her. She turned to face him.

"Where are you—somewhere in your part of the world?" he asked, his eyes traveling over her face.

"*This* is my part of the world now," she replied.

"Do you ever get homesick?"

"A little, sometimes," she admitted. "But not often. I feel at home here."

"Do you think you could be happy here for the rest of your life?" he pursued, a curious, expectant note in his voice.

Jessica shrugged. "I have been, so I don't see why I couldn't."

"But how long do you think you'll be satisfied with the life you have now?"

She frowned and lifted her chin in a gesture that warned him to keep off. "I'm perfectly happy with my life," she said forcefully.

Unheeding, he went on. "Then I don't think you know what perfect happiness is."

"And you're about to tell me?" she said, her voice heavy with sarcasm, her eyes glowing dangerously.

"I'd like to, if you'll let—"

"Really," Jessica interrupted in a voice that cut in like a blade, "you have the most appalling nerve and conceit. How dare—"

With a movement so swift that he gave her no warning, he was out of his chair and leaning across the table toward her. His mouth came down on hers and stopped her in mid-sentence. "We had one hell of a row yesterday. At least give me time to recover from that before we start another," he said against her mouth.

Jessica's spine turned to jelly, and she drew her head feebly back in time to see that every eye in the room had turned with great interest in their direction. Peter, on the other hand, sat down calmly again, oblivious of the stares he had attracted. Horror and a strange thrill clashed inside Jessica as she tried to hide her blazing face by fixing her unseeing eyes on the darkness outside. The thought that he did remember yesterday's quarrel and needed to recover from it was oddly comforting.

"Look," he began again in a conciliatory tone, "what I'm trying to say is, you can't spend the rest of your life in the service of two admittedly very charming but very spoiled women."

"Can't I?" Jessica exploded, her mortification of a moment ago suddenly forgotten. "Well, thank you *so* much for your patronizing interest, but I really—"

"My interest in you is not of a patronizing nature," he cut in with a broad smile. "As I did my best to prove on a couple of occasions."

For a moment this blatant allusion left Jessica speechless and flushed, but her desire to hit back was too strong. "Those two spoiled women, as you call them, are my family, and looking after them is not the life sentence you imply." Pausing for an instant as if taking careful aim at a target, she added, "But then I can't expect you to understand, can I? One failed marriage could hardly have taught you much about family bonds. *You* have no one."

This time he looked silently out of the window. She saw that her words had found their mark, but did not feel the satisfaction she had expected. Looking at his strong profile, devoid of all expression, she regretted her vicious words. He hadn't done anything to provoke such a response from her. Much as she resented what he had said, he had said it out of concern for her.

"I'm sorry," she said quietly. "I had no right to say that."

He turned back to her and, without a trace of affront, said, "Of course you have. You have the right to say anything you want to me. And of course what you say is true—but so is what I say." He held up a warning hand as she opened her mouth to speak and leaned closer to look into her eyes. "Before you jump on me again, let me remind you that a moment ago I found a very enjoyable way to stop your quarreling. So go ahead, get as mad as you like."

Jessica considered his threat and remained silent. Meanwhile the waiter arrived and placed their food before them. Peter waited until the wine had been poured and the waiter had left before speaking again.

"It took me a while to realize what a gutsy girl you are. At first I thought you were just a...well, never mind that, I'll save that for another quarrel," he joked. Then he continued seriously. "I know now how much responsibility you've taken on yourself. I know how hard you work at them. But, like it or not, I have to tell you one thing— I don't think you're doing those women a whole lot of good by pampering them the way you do. No, hear me out. Your sister-in-law should have a career or at least a husband of her own to keep her from growing into a silly, helpless old woman, and your mother-in-law spends too much time mourning the past. She ought to have some other interests in life."

"You have a bloody nerve!" Jessica exclaimed with uncharacteristic coarseness. "I like the arrogant way you're taking it on yourself to rearrange our lives. All this, as I pointed out before, is easy for you to say."

"Not as easy as you think, because I know how much you hate me for saying it."

"Then why say it at all!" she snapped.

"Because..." He hesitated, looking at her with a curious expression. Waiting expectantly, she kept her eyes steady on him, but her breath caught. He shook his head as if to dismiss what he was about to say. "Someone should say it to you. And say it now, because it's going to get harder all the time. Too hard for you alone," he finished.

"You seem to take it for granted that I'll be alone," she retorted, not quite knowing what she meant by the words.

His eyes narrowed, and he gave her a probing look. "You're not hinting at the eligible Mr. Cuttler, are you?"

he asked, his voice taking on a rougher edge.

"It's not my way to hint at such things," Jessica said evasively, pleased to see the smile of assurance leave his face for a change.

Neither of them seemed to be hungry; they'd both been toying with their food. Now Peter put down his knife and fork and stared at Jessica with unwavering speculation. When he spoke at last, his face and voice were tense. "I can believe your protective instincts for the Romneys would drive you to do many things, but marrying a man you don't love for his money wouldn't be one of them, would it?" he demanded.

Jessica stared back at him, a burning spot on each cheek revealing her hurt and indignation. It would have been easy to tell him how she really felt about Eric, but his question—more like a vile accusation—did not warrant an explanation. She looked him steadily in the eyes as she replied coldly, "Naturally, if it was, I wouldn't confide it to *you*."

A muscle in his jaw jumped, and his hand tightened around his wineglass, but he said nothing. He spent the rest of the meal in moody preoccupation.

It was past eleven o'clock when they left the restaurant and strolled out onto the pier. They stood a little apart, leaning over the rail, looking into the still, dark night. Above them the stars of the Southern Cross glowed dimly in the sky. The only sound was the gentle lapping of the waves against the wooden pylons of the pier.

Peter's jacket sleeve brushed against Jessica's bare arm, and she looked up to see that he had moved to her side. Her nerves began to tingle and her heart pounded.

She saw he was about to say something and forestalled him by speaking first. "I'd better get back to the hotel now," she said, her voice sounding strangled to her own ears. "I have a lot to do tomorrow."

"It's still too hot. You won't be able to sleep in that stuffy hotel. Come on, let's have a look at The Gap," he invited.

Beyond Pride 125

Obediently, her heart still performing treacherous acrobatics, she followed him. They climbed the steps of a steep hill to The Gap, the sheer, towering cliff that dropped straight and deadly to the sea hundreds of feet below. At its base giant waves hurled themselves against the rocks in ceaseless violence, sending hissing fountains of spray high into the air. In a city that was generously endowed with scenic beauty, this was one of the most awesomely spectacular sights. The Gap attracted three kinds of people—tourists, lovers, and suicides.

Jessica's hands gripped the safety rail, her hair tossed by the strong breeze off the open sea. She felt his eyes on her, silently, irresistibly drawing her toward him, until she yearned to shut out all their conflicts from her mind and abandon herself to the overpowering need to walk into his arms. Her grip tightened on the rail until her knuckles shone white in the darkness. Peter's hand reached out and came down on hers. Then, as if sensing the pent-up tension in that small white hand, he drew away again.

"Come on," he said quietly. "There's something I want to show you in town."

They drove back to the city in silence. He turned the car toward the banking and business district and parked on a narrow side street beside a block-long fence that protected a great yawning crater.

"Look," he said with a touch of embarrassment, pointing to a large board towering above the fence. Puzzled, she walked closer and read the lettering by the dim street light: "Construction by P. M. Savage Pty. Ltd."

Jessica's face lit up with surprised delight. "That's you!" she cried excitedly. "Are you putting this building up?"

It was the first time she had seen him even remotely embarrassed. His smile was almost boyish as he admitted, "Yeah."

Jessica looked at the site, which gaped between two recently built skyscrapers. "It looks as if it's going to be an important building. What will it be?"

"A bank on the first few floors, above that business offices," he told her, obviously pleased with her enthusiasm. "The excavation is just about finished. That's where I'll come in. We'll start putting down the foundations soon. It's going to be thirty-five stories high."

Jessica craned her neck to imagine how tall the building—his building—would stand. They'd experienced so many shifts of mood between them already tonight that her head whirled. But this was a side of Peter she had never glimpsed before. She couldn't help feeling flattered that he had wanted to share with her something that was obviously important to him, that he seemed eager for her approval.

"It's really awesome," she told him in frank admiration.

"You mean I've succeeded in impressing you at last?" he asked, feigning amazement.

"Yes," she admitted with a smile. "I'm ready to concede that you're a better bricklayer than I am."

"While I have you in a conceding mood, why don't you spend the day with me tomorrow?" His invitation caught her unawares.

"I have too much to do," she said lamely.

"Any of it to do with Eric Cuttler?" he asked. She couldn't see his face well enough to discern his expression, but he'd put the question lightly enough. It would not, she hoped, lead to another hostile exchange. "Eric handles a lot of our business matters," she told him irrelevantly.

He made a disgusted sound. "You know, you'd have a ready-made career if you ever decided to go into politics. I've never known anyone to sidestep a question like you."

"You ask too many questions," she retorted.

"Okay, then, I'll just ask one more. Will you have lunch with me tomorrow?"

"I suppose so," Jessica replied.

On the way back to the hotel, it occurred to Jessica that, although the evening hadn't started out well, for the first time they hadn't ended on a note of animosity.

chapter 10

EARLY THE FOLLOWING DAY, swallowing her pride and steeling herself mentally, Jessica entered the premises of the largest antique jeweler in the city. As she approached the counter, she prayed silently that there would be no fierce or prolonged bargaining involved.

One look at the light in the dealer's eyes as he viewed the pieces, giving especially close scrutiny to the jade, told her she would not have much trouble setting her price. Jade of the quality of the bracelet and earrings was extremely rare—a collector's dream—and the dealer knew at a glance that he would have no trouble reselling them at a great profit. After that the matter was relatively easier, if not less distasteful than Jessica had expected. She left the shop with the satisfaction of having concluded a good bargain, which almost made up for the loss of the treasured pieces. She glanced at the comfortingly fat check that would take care of current emergencies and, with a sigh, placed it in her purse.

She spent the rest of the morning shopping for the small luxuries that made her in-laws' lives bearable. At their favorite beautician she picked up an armful of creams and lotions especially concocted for their sensitive skins. She called at the trichologist who made their special shampoos, searched for the obscure brand of panty hose they preferred, and purchased two large boxes of handmade chocolates.

As she hurried through the teeming streets and

crowded stores, Peter Savage's words of the night before returned to her. Was he right? Was she, in fact, doing the wrong thing pampering and shielding Iris and Carlotta? Would her protection of them be more harmful than kind in the long run? Reluctantly she admitted that what Peter said sometimes made sense. Maybe.

Suddenly a picture flashed into Jessica's mind of the three of them twenty years from now. The image made her stop in her tracks with a shudder, then hurry on as if she were being pursued.

At the end of the long, busy morning she headed back to her hotel, exhausted. It was another steaming hot day in Sydney. The unseasonable heat wave that had arrived in October still held. By midmorning the temperature had soared into the nineties and the city was bathed in a sticky, stifling vapor of humidity. Though Christmas was more than a month away, the rush on the shops had already begun, and Jessica, weighed down with parcels, had to weave her way carefully through jostling crowds.

She reached the haven of her room gratefully and immediately stripped to her underwear and kicked off her shoes. She collapsed on the bed and closed her eyes. In a half hour it would be time to get ready for her lunch date with Peter, and she could not deny the unbidden excitement with which she anticipated their meeting. Slowly she let herself drift into a light sleep.

Twenty minutes later she awoke with a start in the stiflingly hot room, her body covered with a film of perspiration. She took a lukewarm shower, rubbed herself dry, then splashed on cologne. From the wardrobe she took the light blue-green sleeveless dress she had worn on her train trip and examined it critically. It still looked crisp and uncrushed, its color especially flattering to her green eyes. She piled her still-damp hair onto the top of her head to leave her neck cool and free, then added some light touches of makeup. Any more would melt right off her face in this heat. It was suffocating in the room, and she knew it would be like a furnace outside.

Beyond Pride

Peter was waiting in the lobby, looking unwilted in cream-colored slacks and a pale gray shirt open at the neck. A navy blazer was swung carelessly over one shoulder.

He leaned close when she came up to him and sniffed at her exposed neck, his breath against her skin raising tiny goose bumps there. "Delicious," he said with a long intake of breath, as if enjoying a flower. "Where can I take you to show you off?"

"Somewhere so cold it'll make my teeth chatter," she requested, though a small shiver had already passed through her at his nearness. She glanced distractedly out at the street, where the heat was shimmering visibly on the sidewalk.

"I know just the place. We'll go somewhere nearby to save driving about in this heat," he decided.

They drove a few blocks to one of the city's tallest buildings and parked in the underground garage. In the elevator the blessed cool of air conditioning enveloped them. They rode to the top floor, to the famous revolving restaurant.

"It's a bit touristy but the food is good, it's cool, and I can point out to you some of the buildings I've worked on. Do you mind?" he asked.

"No, I love it. I've never been here," she assured him, looking about the circular room with its lush carpets, beautifully set tables, hurrying waiters, and luxuriously hushed atmosphere.

There were shown to a deep, cushiony banquette before one of the floor-to-ceiling windows. Outside, the city, the harbor, and the surrounding countryside lay sprawled below them. Buildings that had looked so tall from the ground seemed dwarfed by the restaurant's great height. Jessica felt as if they were floating on a cool remote cloud over the heat and bustle of the city.

She relaxed as she sipped at the frosty drink the waiter had placed at her elbow. As the room revolved almost imperceptibly, Peter pointed to one building after another that he had helped put up, either as a laborer or later as a contractor. They lunched lightly on salads and sipped more tall, cool drinks.

"Would you like to live in a building like this?" Peter asked, following her fascinated glance out the window.

"No," she answered after a moment's hesitation. "It's splendid, but I could never feel at home here. I like being close to the ground."

"Yeah," he joked. "First thing I noticed about you was that you were the earthy type."

Jessica ignored this crack and continued. "I'd miss too many things up here. You'd never see a tree, or hear birds, or smell freshly cut grass."

He made a sound of surprise that drew her attention. "Who would have thought it," he remarked. "The woman's a romantic."

"What about you?" she asked.

"I'm one, too," he confessed.

Not from her experience, she thought, but aloud she said, "No, I mean would you like to live in a place like this?"

"I have a home, and I wouldn't change it for all the penthouses and all the views in the world." In his usual disconcerting way he looked straight at her, making it sound as if there was something hidden behind his words.

Jessica's eyes wavered and sought refuge outside the window. The room had now turned away from the harbor and was facing the Blue Mountains, far in the distance to the west. "But once you start working on that site you showed me last night, you won't be able to commute from Sommerville every day," she pointed out.

"I have a small beach place where I stay when I'm in Sydney. Why don't you come and see it?"

"I don't—" Jessica began automatically to devise an excuse, but he forestalled her.

"If you're going to tell me you have business to take care of, I want to remind you it's close to a hundred degrees out there now. My place is on the water. You could swim, or I could take you for a spin in the boat."

Jessica thought of the blasting heat of the city streets.

Walking about them was out of the question. The alternative of going back to the tiny sweatbox that was her hotel room was also unthinkable. By contrast the picture he had conjured up was hard to resist. She loved the sea.

Last night she and Peter had managed to be quite civil to each other, and, apart from that swift kiss in the restaurant, he hadn't touched her. All through lunch he had been unusually courteous. Perhaps, she pondered, their relationship was taking a less hostile turn. She accepted his invitation.

Soon they were heading out of the city toward the north bypass that led onto the Harbour Bridge. As always, no matter how many times she crossed this bridge, Jessica was filled with awe at the magnificence of the harbor it spanned. She craned her neck as they passed the billowing white sail shapes of the Sydney Opera House, standing against a cloudless blue sky over to their right. Sailboats dotted the sparkling water below, and from Circular Quay ferries churned their slow, stately way across to the northern shores.

The heat rose around them in scorching blasts, so fierce it made Jessica's eyes burn and her throat feel dry. They drove through the busy commercial center of North Sydney toward the northern beaches. At one of the byroads Peter turned off the highway and drove through quiet tree-lined streets of neat brick-and-timber houses to the water's edge. Squeezing the car through a narrow back lane, he parked behind one of the houses fronting the sea. A small gate in the fence led them into a tiny back garden. From here Jessica could see a path leading past the front of the house straight onto the sandy shore of a small inlet.

The house itself was a small, plain structure of timber and glass, painted a dazzling white with navy blue trim and shutters. The entire front was glassed in to make a sunroom and sleeping porch. The inside was divided evenly by a narrow hallway with three small bedrooms on one side and a living room, kitchen, and bathroom on the other. The rooms were sparsely furnished, mostly in cane and rattan, and the whole house looked neat, clean, and cool—a complete contrast to the grandeur of Romney House.

The cottage was stuffy after weeks of disuse, and Peter immediately opened every window, keeping the shutters closed and turning on ceiling fans. At his invitation Jessica explored the house. The back bedroom contained a drafting table and instruments she guessed were connected with the business of architecture and engineering. She pictured Peter bending over the table, his strong hands capably handling the instruments. Once again she had the feeling that she was glimpsing an unfamiliar side of him.

She was completely captivated by the small, neat, unpretentious house even before she saw the view. From the shaded sun porch she could see the entire small inlet on which the house stood. A private beach directly in front was shared by the five or six other houses. To the right, past the mouth of the tiny bay, Jessica could see a stretch of open sea, while to the left was a bush-covered cliff, part of a nature preserve.

The ocean lapped gently onto the sand, its sight and sound a cooling, refreshing promise. Hot and dizzy from the heat, she would have given anything to rush in headlong.

Peter stood beside her. "Why don't you go for a swim?"

"I have nothing to wear," she said with regret, her eyes on the water.

He took her measure thoughtfully for a moment and then walked back into the house. "Wait, I might have something for you," he called from the hall.

Jessica's spirits took an unexpected dive. Was he one of those men who kept an array of women's swimsuits around just in case, she thought with resentment. If he thought she would wear castoffs from an old girlfriend...

A moment later he was back, holding out to her what looked like one of his own T-shirts. "That's the best I can do. Think you can use it?" he asked apologetically.

"Oh, yes!" Jessica exclaimed, her spirits reviving.

In one of the bedrooms she took off her dress and stood before a mirror in her blue silk, lace-trimmed panties and bra. She pulled on the black, short-sleeved T-shirt, which promptly plunged to her knees. Hesitating for a moment, she peered in the mirror. It wasn't all that flattering, but at least it was a very chaste garment, she decided.

When Peter saw her, he gave a long, raucous whistle. "Miss Bondi Beach, 1911," he commented, shaking his head regretfully. "If only my shirts were ten sizes smaller—"

"I wouldn't be wearing one of them," she finished for him.

He gave her a lopsided grin. "Go ahead, dive in. I'll get some towels and change myself." He disappeared inside.

Jessica ran for the water. Her first contact with a wave was an icy shock, but in another moment she plunged in headlong, and her body became accustomed to the cold. She dived and swam and floated, completely abandoning herself to the invigorating waves.

Soon Peter's head bobbed up beside her. They treaded water silently.

"Have you had this house long?" Jessica asked him after a while.

"About eight years," he replied lazily and took a sudden dive to surface on her other side. "It was the first place I ever bought. Just a two-room shack then. I added the rest myself."

"It's a lovely little house." Jessica sighed, floating on the water in blissful abandonment, her arms outstretched, her hair streaming out behind her. "It's perfect. So private."

"It's yours any time you want to use it."

Jessica stole a glance at him. He was such a puzzle to her. To think that the same man who could be so contemptuously, so ruthlessly blunt one minute could shower her with such extravagant generosity the next.

"That's kind of you," she told him, "but the chances of me making use of it are pretty remote. Iris and Carlotta don't care for the beach and—" She stopped at the impatient sound he made. He gave her a look full of meaning and swam away in long, powerful strokes. She was reminded of their conversation the night before and winced. It really did sound as if she didn't make a move without first considering her in-laws.

Suddenly chilled, she headed for the beach. As she stood up in shallow water, the T-shirt clung heavily to her body. Rivulets of water ran from the hem, which had ridden high up on her thighs. She looked in consternation at the way the wet shirt molded itself to her, outlining every detail of her underwear. She glanced behind her in alarm to see Peter assessing her with a bold, unwavering stare. A smile flashed across his face at her embarrassment as he came out of the water.

"Here," he said with an elaborate show of turning away, throwing her a towel. "Hide yourself in that."

Jessica's embarrassment gave way to humiliated anger. His amused glance had made her feel like an immature girl. She stared resentfully at his tanned back, and with a swift movement pulled off the shirt and hurled it at him. It landed with a wet smack and made him turn around in surprise, just as she was securing the towel around her.

"Care to try for the towel too?" he challenged, giving a low, mocking laugh at the expression on her face. She walked over to one of two deck chairs he had placed side by side on the sand while he went inside to make drinks.

It was now late afternoon, but the sun was still as fierce as if it had been noon. Jessica stretched out in the chair, her eyes closed against the glare. As the sun warmed her sea-chilled body and caressed her skin she became languid and drowsily relaxed. A little later she opened her eyes to the clinking of ice beside her and found Peter standing there holding a tall glass out to her. The sight of his tall, lean body flashing golden in the

Beyond Pride 137

sunlight took her breath away. He sat down in the chair beside hers and took a swallow from his drink. She, too, drank thirstily from the light, refreshing liquid, her hands trembling faintly. She no longer felt languid and relaxed. She was far too aware of the long, hard body stretched out beside her.

When the sun became too hot again, she squirmed uncomfortably, feeling sticky from the salt on her skin, her damp underwear clinging steamily to her.

"Could I take a shower, please?" she asked.

The eyes that had been half closed, looking into the distance, flew open, and she was struck by their startling blueness. "I've put some towels out for you in the bathroom. I think you'll find everything else you need there. When you've finished, look in my closet for another shirt or something to put on. I'd like to take you for a spin in the boat to show you some of the coastline around here. It gets a bit messy in the boat, so don't put your dress on."

In the bathroom Jessica stripped off and rinsed out her underwear, then lay it on the sun-warm window sill to dry.

She glanced about the bathroom, feeling a sense of intimacy looking at Peter's shaving things on the shelf. He had laid out fresh soap, a bottle of shampoo, and a new toothbrush for her. Everything was a masculine brand. There was not the least evidence that he ever had women guests.

Jessica reveled in the shower for a long time, then wrapped a towel around her and tiptoed out to the porch. Peter was waist deep in the bay, tinkering with the engine of a small speedboat.

Reassured, she went to his room and opened the closet, feeling a strange bond of familiarity with this man she had known less than two months. She selected a worn blue work shirt that didn't look as if it would be spoiled by a lively boat ride.

Back in the bathroom she slipped on her dry underthings, towel-dried her hair, and applied fresh makeup.

She put on Peter's work shirt and looked at herself in the mirror. It reached to her knees, looking more like a loose-fitting dress than a shirt.

Outside Peter, still bent over the boat, saw her come out of the house and straightened up to look her over. "You can have the shirt off my back anytime," he declared after making a thorough scrutiny. "It looks a whole lot better on you."

Trying to ignore his compliment, although her pulse seemed unusually light and fast, Jessica waded out to where the boat was bobbing up and down in thigh-high water. With one effortless move Peter scooped her up in his arms and dropped her into the boat, then climbed in beside her. Her indignant protests went ignored as he maneuvered the boat carefully through the shallows and around numerous rocks until they were out of the inlet and on the open sea. He increased the power until the engine roared, and the boat shot forward in a spray of churned water, fairly flying across the surface.

Jessica sat on a cushioned seat in the stern, feeling a thrill surge through her as the air rushed past them and the boat lifted from the water on the crest of each succeeding wave. She watched both the fleeting shoreline and Peter Savage, his bare feet firmly planted, his hands effortlessly controlling the wheel, with equal fascination. He half turned and summoned her to his side.

"Take the wheel," he ordered, raising his voice over the roar of the boat.

"I've never handled one of these before," she protested, but he pulled her in front of him and placed her hands on the wheel.

"You'll get the hang of it in no time," he said close to her ear, standing behind her, his arms around her as he guided her hands.

His chest burned into her back more powerfully than the heat of the sun. With each lurch of the boat she was thrown hard against him, and he steadied her with an encircling arm. She tried to hold herself rigidly so she wouldn't move against him, but the commanding rhythm of the boat's movement was irresistible, and she soon found herself responding to it on sure feet.

In a surprisingly short time Jessica began to get the feel of the boat, and Peter let her take over completely. She felt a wild exhilaration as she directed the speeding craft on its flight on the open stretch of sea. She braced herself against the onrush of wind and water and felt as if there were nothing beneath her feet, as if she had become airborne. They passed miles of open coastline and sheltered small bays before Peter put his hands over hers once more.

"Ease her along to the left here," he commanded. "There's a cove I want to show you." As they neared the shore, he took over the controls and gingerly edged the boat into a tiny, shallow bay, skirting around an outcrop of reef to the gaping mouth of a cave half submerged in water. It was so concealed by surrounding rocks that it wasn't visible from the open sea.

The cave was high and sun filtered through holes in its ceiling, sending shafts of light into its emerald depths. The filtered light and the green reflection from the water gave it the soft, silent gloom of a cathedral.

"Oh, it's beautiful!" Jessica breathed as Peter nudged the boat through the entrance. "And look, it's quite unspoiled by human hands. No graffiti on the walls, no beer cans bobbing about."

"I don't think many people know about it. I discovered it by accident a couple of years ago when I was looking for a spot to fish."

"I hope no one else finds it," she replied, suddenly jealous of the beautiful, hidden spot that was his alone.

"We'll keep it to ourselves," he said softly.

Jessica's eyes were drawn to his. She saw something quicken there and instinctively began to draw away, but his arms were already encircling her, forcing her resisting body against his until she was forced to yield to his strength. The hard collision of their bodies gave her an urgent warning that in a minute it would be too late, and she made a last attempt to avoid his kiss by jerking her head back out of his reach. His mouth came down on her throat, and she felt his lips searing against her skin. The sound that escaped her acted as a signal to him. He grasped the hair at the nape of her neck and twisted her face to his. For an instant before his mouth found hers she saw his face—tense, hard, a frightening, stranger's face. His kiss held no tenderness. Her ineffectual struggle only roused a more relentless response from him.

Irrelevantly, somewhere in the back of her mind, she wondered why a kiss was supposed to bring chills to one's spine. Her own had lost all its power to support her. Her knees sagged as if her legs were about to give way under her. Slowly Peter lowered her to the bottom of the boat, his lips never leaving hers. The work shirt rode up over her thighs, and its gaping collar slid down over her shoulder. His mouth claimed the exposed shoulder, his hand working the shirt further down until she was uncovered to the waist save for the flimsy protection of her bra. His hand traveled further in a gesture so possessively intimate that it shocked even her unresisting senses.

With a strength born of sheer panic, she twisted away. A sound—half sob, half groan—escaped her. It stopped him in mid-motion. He stared at her, his eyes dark with passion, then abruptly let her go and jumped to his feet. With a last look at her, a look that mingled scorn with hopelessness, he returned to the wheel. With less care than he had eased it in, he headed the boat out of the cove.

chapter 11

ON THE TRIP back Jessica sat huddled in the stern as far from him as possible. Not once did he turn to look at her. There was an eloquence in the way the muscles of his back were rigidly tensed, in the way he gripped the wheel. She looked at the shoreline as they drew near, trying to fix her thoughts on something other than the misery welling up inside her.

If not for her self-deceptive weakness, this would never have happened, she accused herself ruthlessly. Had she really been able to convince herself that their relationship had taken a different turn? Had he even wanted to believe that when she had so readily accepted his invitation? This time she had no right to feel indignant toward him—coming here had taken that right away. She could only feel contempt for herself.

She dwelled on the bitter irony of having fled Sommerville two days before to escape a situation she couldn't face, only to hurl herself headlong into another, much more serious one. She had known then that her relationship with him had gone irretrievably beyond that of mere neighbors, just as she had known when she'd agreed to spend a day alone with him in his house.

She raised a shaking hand to her head and stared at his unresponsive back in humiliation. How could she face him after this? Conflicting emotions tormented her. She shrank from becoming involved with him, from the intimacy that he was demanding. But all the while his kisses still burned in her blood.

When Peter nosed the boat into the inlet and stopped it near the beach, Jessica clambered out awkwardly before he had a chance to help her and rushed into the house. Her one thought was to leave as quickly as possible. Once she was far away from here she would be able to think clearly again, put the whole thing in perspective.

In the guest bedroom she tore off Peter's shirt and pulled on her dress. Hastily she stepped into her sandals and snatched her purse up. With a last wild look about, she turned to go.

He was standing in the doorway, his body blocking it. She made a move toward him, her voice rising out of control. "I want to go now!"

Without moving, he stood staring at her, the cold fire of his gaze burning into her. His face was drawn and his jaw set rigidly, but his voice was sure and calm. "No, you don't want to leave."

He spoke so matter-of-factly, with such absolute certainty, that humiliation and anger flared in her. She had betrayed herself so completely that he dared speak to her like this.

"No, you don't want to go," he repeated, moving away from the door as if to prove his point by making the way clear for her to leave. His calm voice became harsher. "You pride yourself on being able to handle anything. Can you handle this truth—that you want to stay with me?"

"The truth as *you* see it," Jessica lashed out, digging her fingers into her palms to keep tears of rage and shame from her eyes.

He shook his head and came closer, his eyes piercing and relentless. "The truth as we *both* know it—as we knew it not half an hour ago, as we knew it back in Sommerville, as I think we've both known it almost from the beginning."

Jessica stood looking at him wordlessly, unable to deny what he was saying.

His voice rose for a moment, losing its calmness.

Beyond Pride

"The thing you can't stand, the thing that makes you look at me with such hatred now is that I treat you like a woman, not as some"—he searched for the right word—"some object of reverence. And I'd bet anything that I'm the first man ever to do that."

Jessica fought to steady her lips before she could reply. "If you mean you're the first man in my experience who completely separates sex from every other emotion, you're absolutely right!" She saw something flinch in his face for a moment, and he started to speak, but she was determined not to let him. She was filled with an icy, steely anger, a need to hurt him the way he had hurt her. She couldn't control her own feelings, couldn't hide them from him. But at least she could make him see in what contempt she held them, make him see she could match his cynical view of their relationship.

A sudden recklessness seized her, and her eyes held a feverish light as she stepped before him. The words came in a defiant, bitter rush. "All right, I'll be as honest as you suggest. I admit that I'm attracted to you... in a most contemptible, physical way." She paused for a moment to measure the effect of her words, but his expression betrayed no emotion. She continued ruthlessly. "It's not the way I have ever felt about any man before, not the way I ever want to feel again. And yes, you're right, I don't want to go. I'll spend the night with you if you want. Is that explicitly truthful enough for you? Is that what you wanted to hear from me?" she challenged.

She saw the flicker of something akin to pain cross his eyes, a hesitancy as if he was fighting an inner struggle. But in a moment it was gone, and his face was devoid of all expression once again.

"It will do—for now," he replied quietly.

Jessica stood rigid but unresisting as he bent over her. She let him kiss her mouth, her eyes, her throat. Still passive, she allowed him to undress her. She fixed her eyes on a far point, trying to detach herself from the sensations that began to stir in her as his lips and hands took fervent, demanding, bold possession of her. With a deep, ragged breath he tore himself away to look at her naked body, and she felt as if every inch of it was on fire under his hungry gaze. She shuddered with a feverish chill under this exposure, until he enfolded her again and forced her mouth open to his. Involuntarily her arms flew around his neck, and she was no longer able to deny the tormenting passion that was flooding her. She strained against him in a burst of desire too long kept in check.

He laid her on the bed, and his movements held little tenderness as he crushed her under him in merciless possession. His mouth left its scorching brand on her breasts, circling the taut nipples with his tongue until she arched beneath him, seeking to draw him ever closer to her. His lips trailed a burning path down the length of her body, and she turned her face into the pillow, entwining her fingers in his hair to stop him. But he wouldn't let her hide her pleasure and, twisting her head, forced her to face him. Their eyes met and remained locked during the next moments of rising passion, their every emotion bared to each other. Jessica trembled at such intimacy, every secret, every thread of unbearable tension she was feeling revealed to him. Still he forced her to meet his eyes as he moved over her to take full and final possession of her. And in that moment of her most helpless surrender, she saw her feelings mirrored in his own face and exulted in her power over him. And then they were moving together, oblivious to everything but the waves of desire rising to a devastating crescendo between them. The world fell away, and they lay spent and gasping in each other's arms.

Slowly their breathing subsided to a calmer rhythm. They untangled arms and legs, lying side by side, gently touching. Peter's arm curved above Jessica's head in a protective gesture, and her hand lay nestled on his chest just above his heart.

Finally he rose to look at her, propping himself up on an elbow. He bent over her, his expression relaxed, his vivid blue eyes soft with a tenderness she had never seen in them before. The gentle kisses he showered onto her mouth and into the palms of her hands were an unexpected aftermath of the almost savage passion that had gone before. He propped himself higher to look at her body again, his gaze lingering on her without the distracting urgency of desire.

"Sweet," he murmured in her ear. "Beautiful and sweet."

Jessica stretched joyously, luxuriating under his caressing stare. She waited for regret or shame to come now that her mind was clear, but instead she felt elated, curiously liberated by her complete abandonment. There was no self-consciousness, no restraint in the way she offered her lovely, slender body to his eyes. She closed her eyes and took his murmured endearments as her due, a half smile on her lips. A sense of relief washed over her, as if a burden of dishonesty had just been lifted from her soul. The moments she had just spent were some of the most natural and truthful she had ever known.

She opened her eyes and met his gaze. He was staring at her with a frown of wonder, and she guessed that he too had been shaken by something beyond passion in their union.

After a while he brought a pile of extra pillows from another bedroom, propped her up on them comfortably, then got a glass of wine for each of them. Jessica followed his every movement, taking pleasure in the sight of his body that was suddenly so familiar to her. They sipped their wine and spoke quietly of small, inconsequential matters while the room grew gradually dark about them.

Finally Peter reached to switch on a small bedside lamp. "I'm a lousy host for not asking before, but are you hungry?"

Jessica shook her head.

"Just as well," he said. "I don't think there's a thing to eat in the house. The cupboard's completely bare." With a significant grin he added, "Just goes to show you this whole thing was not premeditated."

"Wasn't it?" she asked with a doubting smile.

He laughed. "All right, I'm lying. I've been meditating it since the first time I saw you." He put down his glass and leaned over to kiss her, his lips at first lightly touching hers, then growing more insistent. Jessica returned the kiss, then sprang off the bed.

"Where are you going?" he cried in alarm.

"Outside for a breath of fresh air," she called over her shoulder as she walked down the hall.

She stood for a moment on the dark porch, unselfconsciously naked, feeling a sensuous freedom in having her body exposed to the balmy night breeze. All around her the bay lay in darkness except for the remote glow of lights from several other houses.

Slowly, taking pleasure in every daring step, she crossed the stretch of sand to the water's edge, paused for an instant, and then plunged into the waves. The cold water on her naked skin produced both shock and ecstasy. She swam with strong, vigorous strokes across the inlet to an outcropping of rock and heaved herself out of the water. She stood with her feet apart, her arms stretched over her head, facing the open sea, her back to the small beach. She felt a wild exhilaration, her body so alive that she was conscious of each separate nerve in it. The breeze stirred her hair and caressed her naked skin, making her even more intensely aware of her body. She thought of Peter's body, of him waiting for her at the house, and a freshly awakened thrill shot through her. Quickly she dove back into the water and swam toward the beach again. When she was near, she saw him at the water's edge watching her. He had a towel around his waist and was holding another for her.

When she was quite near he called out in a low, amused voice, "You're a scandal, Jessica. I don't know how I'll be able to hold my head up again in this community. I have to warn you that one of my neighbors is a bloke from the vice squad."

"Am I embarrassing you?" she asked hopefully.

"What you're causing me couldn't be further from embarrassment," he replied in a thick voice. Throwing off his own towel, he waded out to her. They stood in waist-deep water, Jessica's glistening breasts rising and falling after the exertion of her swim and with an excitement stirring in her. Peter touched her breasts lightly, his own breath coming fast and unevenly. They met in an embrace so urgent that it dragged them off their feet and down to the sandy bottom of the water. When they surfaced, Jessica gasped for air.

"This calls for mouth-to-mouth resuscitation," Peter said, picking her up and carrying her to the beach, where he lay her down on the sand. "Don't worry, I learned all about it in the Boy Scouts," he murmured before lying full length on top of her and applying his own special technique.

Struggling to her elbows between his kisses, Jessica said weakly, "Must have been a very advanced course of lifesaving they were teaching you boys."

"Keep still, I haven't demonstrated the half of it," he replied against her mouth.

She became oblivious to everything,—the cold discomfort of the sand beneath her, the open sky overhead, everything but his hard, wet body covering hers, rousing her to fresh madness.

Suddenly he stood up and scooped her up into his arms. "I'm all for being one with nature," he told her in a thick whisper, "but if I don't take you inside, the mosquitoes will play havoc with your luscious little behind. An unromantic detail to consider at a time like this, I know, but you'll thank me for it in the morning."

"You think of everything." She smiled into his eyes.

Inside they lay side by side, and this time it was Jessica who drew back to look at him and touch him, at first tentatively, then more knowingly and surely. With proud satisfaction she felt the tremors passing through the strong body under her hand. They made love again, this time more tenderly and lingeringly, with no conflict between them. Afterward she lay in his arms, enveloped in a calm bliss that wiped all the bitter words and doubts out of existence.

A long while later, when each of them had showered, they sat on the screened porch wrapped in sheets, sipping wine and talking. When it was well past midnight Jessica admitted to a gnawing hunger, and they went fishing. Peter opened a small can of prawns for bait, brought his rods in from the garage, and took her in a small dinghy to a spot where he knew the fish were eager to bite. In a half hour they had caught five leatherjackets, tough-skinned but deliciously tender small, flat fish. At home he cleaned them expertly and grilled them with a light coating of oil, flour, salt, and pepper. They ate the crisp, flavorful pieces with pickles and canned Camembert they'd discovered deep in one of the kitchen cupboards.

Back on the porch again, they lay side by side in deck chairs, talking easily or just as easily lapsing into comfortable silence. Now and then Jessica caught Peter looking at her in a curiously musing, uncertain way that was so unlike his usual bold, assured appraisal. She wondered if something was on his mind, but if so, he was too wary to confide it to her. Could he, in his own way, be as full of doubt about her as she was about him?

She didn't dare examine her own feelings. This night with him had been so splendid, such an unexpected gift, that she was terrified of spoiling it with a wayward thought.

When a faint light began to touch the horizon, Jessica felt as fresh and awake as if she had slept through the night. She and Peter watched the gradual, spectacular awakening of the world around them, and when the sun had finally, fully risen, Jessica stood up and stretched languorously.

Peter reached out to take her hand. "Stay with me here a few days, then we can go back together," he suggested.

Jessica sighed and shook her head. "No, I promised I'd be home by tonight."

"Then just stay today, and I'll drive you home tonight."

Like a rude awakening, Jessica remembered her appointment with Eric. If only there was some way she could get out of it. For a moment she considered calling him and canceling their lunch date. But she remembered he had said he wanted to discuss something important. Besides, she wouldn't be so rude as to cancel at the last minute.

She shook her head. "I can't. I have some things to take care of in town first."

"I'll help you do them, or I'll wait until you're finished, then I'll drive you back. We can fly in a chopper if you like."

"I have a lunch date." She flushed hotly despite herself, and in an instant his soft expression vanished.

"I don't have to ask if it's with Eric Cuttler, I suppose," he said harshly.

"Well, yes it is..." she began. His face reflected anger and disgust, and not a hint of what had passed between them in the last hours.

Peter's eyes held an impenetrable coldness as he spoke. "You made it pretty clear when you made your little speech last night that you didn't mean to get overly sentimental over this whole affair. But climbing out of my bed to keep a lunch date with Cuttler is a little blasé, wouldn't you say?" he asked savagely.

Jessica stared at him as if struck. What had happened? What could have passed in a few minutes to destroy a whole night? After what they had shared, how could he speak to her like this? His words, the cold mask of his face, made her reel with pain.

It just proved one thing, she told herself bitterly. If a few words could so devastatingly wipe out all that had happened between them, then it had been nothing more than a physical attraction that had cooled the moment the last embrace was over. She fought down the hurt before she replied as coolly as she could manage, "You put it just as crudely as the whole thing merits."

He would not allow her to call for a taxi but insisted on driving her back himself. The trip was torture for Jessica, and she called on every ounce of will power to keep from breaking down. Several times she considered telling Peter the truth about Eric, but each time pride held her back.

When they arrived at her hotel, he let her out without a word and drove off without a backward glance.

chapter 12

WHEN JESSICA ARRIVED at the restaurant they had decided on two days before, Eric was already waiting for her. He pulled a chair out for her.

"I'm glad you could make it. I was surprised when Iris told me the other night that you'd come up to town and I hadn't heard from you."

"I'm sorry, Eric, it's just that I had so much to do in the short time I planned to stay here," she apologized with a guilty flush.

Eric peered at her closely. "I think you've been overdoing it, Jessica. You look terribly worn out. You've got dark circles under your eyes."

Jessica's flush deepened painfully, and she escaped behind the large menu the waiter had placed before her. "Oh, you know how hot it's been," she muttered.

"Yes, and I know you don't spare yourself," he said. "You've taken too much on yourself since Roderick ... well, that's partly what I wanted to talk to you about. But first let's eat. Shall I order for you?"

Jessica glanced at him uneasily. He sounded a little nervous, and she wondered with a moment's apprehension whether he was about to make advances to her again. But no, Eric wasn't the type of man to press his suit once it had been turned down.

She sat patiently while he ordered extensively and rather fussily in French. Apart from the mental distress that she was trying to keep in check, she was also battling physical exhaustion. She hoped she could get through lunch without either bursting into tears or falling asleep across the table.

They chatted, over their meal, and again Jessica noted that Eric looked unusually ill-at-ease. He brought up the financial matters that had been the pretext for the lunch, but he failed to give them his usual astute attention.

Jessica had been listlessly picking at the food on her plate throughout the meal and was relieved when the waiter finally took the barely touched dish away. When their coffee came, Eric at last cleared his throat, his usual signal that he was about to speak of something significant. He fumbled with his cuff links and flashed her a nervous smile.

"I'm glad we've remained friends despite... well, you know..."

Jessica put out a hand and patted his arm with understanding.

"Getting back to what I began to say earlier, you must start accepting more practical help from me from now on. You see, I believe that soon the concerns of the Romneys will be as much mine as yours. Am I making sense?" he asked uncertainly.

Puzzled, she shook her head. "Not yet. Why don't you try again?" she suggested.

"The thing is... what I really want to tell you is that, though I have known Iris all her life, it wasn't until recently that..." He stopped and looked helplessly at her. Understanding began to dawn, and the smile she flashed him gave him the courage to go on. "...that I started to feel differently about her. I think she feels the same. I decided it would be a good idea if we got married," he blurted out in a rush, then looked at Jessica with a worried expression.

Jessica jumped to her feet and kissed his forehead impulsively. "Oh Eric, that's wonderful! I'm so happy."

Eric basked in her congratulations before a doubtful frown creased his face. "I haven't actually, formally asked her yet, you know... but I have hopes she'll accept. Do you think she will?" he asked anxiously.

Jessica suppressed a knowing smile as she recalled her sister-in-law's clearly stated plans to capture Eric Cuttler. "I think so. I happen to know she's crazy about you." The doubt disappeared from his face.

"I'm told you can never be certain with women, but even so, I bought this," he said, pulling a small velvet box from his pocket and placing it before Jessica. Inside the small scarlet nest was a ring with an enormous sapphire surrounded by diamonds.

Jessica gasped with awe. "It's magnificent. Oh, I can't tell you how happy I am for you both. I think you'll be wonderfully happy. And you say Iris doesn't know about this yet? I can't wait to get home. When are you returning to Sommerville?"

"Well, to tell you the truth," Eric admitted with more excitement than his usual formality allowed, "I'm rather impatient to see Iris myself. Since you're returning today, why don't we go together?"

For a moment Jessica remembered a similar offer she had received earlier that day and felt a small stab of pain. How differently things might have turned out. But she was too happy for Iris to linger over that regret for long. Buoyed with new energy, she said, "My bag is already packed. I just have to call at the hotel to get it."

"In that case, let's go right now! We can be there before dinner. Waiter, our bill, please!" Eric cried with the impatience of a true lover. Jessica laughed at him affectionately. Considering the way she'd felt when Peter had dropped her at her hotel, she wouldn't have believed it possible to feel such gladness so soon.

They reached Sommerville in the early evening, while it was still light. Eric's excited talk of his plans for the future and Jessica's fatigue had kept her mind numb during the trip. But when they approached the outskirts of town, her heart began to hammer. She wondered if Peter had returned before her, or if he had stayed on in Sydney.

Eric's plans for the future had carried a sure note of

confidence throughout the long drive, but as he parked at the side of the road, he looked anxiously at Jessica. "You know, I've been taking things rather for granted. The truth is that, beyond a few hints and talking about it in a rather general way, I've never actually discussed marriage with Iris. Now I wonder if she'll..." His voice trailed off uncertainly.

"I have a feeling you're going to be an engaged man when we sit down to dinner tonight," Jessica hastily reassured him.

"You think so? Think she'll accept? Lord, I've never made an actual proposal to anyone before."

Jessica laughed and put a comforting hand on his shoulder. At that moment a Jeep passed and abruptly slowed down on the other side of the road. Though she couldn't see his face, she recognized the fair hair. For an instant her heart filled with hope, then the Jeep took off with a furious roar and sped away. It was obvious that Peter had seen them, and obvious how he had interpreted what he'd seen.

Eric was too engrossed in his own problems to have noticed anything, and as he went on talking about the forthcoming proposal with growing confidence, Jessica half listened with a stricken mind. Every circumstance seemed to conspire to widen the gap of misunderstanding between herself and Peter. Her one comfort was that he would soon hear of the engagement and learn the truth. Then he would know how unnecessary and unfair his words had been to her.

In the last, turbulent twenty-four hours she seemed to have lived through a whole range of emotions. Her fatigue began to have a paralyzing effect on her, and only the prospect of seeing Iris and Carlotta's happiness kept her going.

Jessica had telephoned ahead to let them know she and Eric would be returning home together, and when they turned in at the cottage gate the two women were already waiting for them on the veranda. One look at the sheepish expression on Eric's face seemed to be enough

Beyond Pride

for Iris. She gave Jessica a secret, knowing glance and linked a proprietary arm through his.

On the pretext that she had some purchases to show Carlotta, Jessica hustled her upstairs to her room. In a surprisingly short time there was a knock on the door, and a radiant Iris made her entrance.

This was a dramatic moment, unequaled by any in her life thus far, and Iris made the most of it. She took her place center stage, clasped her hands before her, and in a suitably hushed and tearful voice announced, "Mother, Jessica, I am engaged!"

Jessica rushed to embrace her, but Carlotta remained standing as if rooted to the spot, a look of disbelief making her look almost comical.

"To whom?" she asked in a fearful voice.

Iris took her cue magnificently. "To Eric Cuttler," she announced and waited as if expecting thunderous applause. Then, dropping all pretense, she squealed excitedly. "Look!" she cried, flashing the sapphire-and-diamond ring under her mother's nose.

Carlotta kept staring incredulously from Iris to Jessica. Her thoughts were clear to the others. Iris and Eric had known each other most of their lives, yet had never shown the slightest romantic inclination. Only when she had looked at Jessica long enough to receive a silent, understanding reassurance from her that she felt no hurt or disappointment, only delight, did Carlotta allow herself to respond.

"Darling, that's too wonderful!" she exclaimed, throwing her arms around her daughter. "I had no idea. You and Eric—how long? Really, I couldn't be more surprised. Oh, delighted, of course. Iris darling, what a superb stone. It must be at least fifteen carats. Darling, you're going to have the *most* divine wedding, not like that nasty registry office thing you had in London—no wonder it didn't last. Eric Cuttler! When did it all happen? Does his mother know? Won't she be just *too* livid when she learns that I heard first," she poured out in a breathless torrent of words. "Oh, where *is* Eric? I must go and see the dear boy at once!" She left the room in search of her future son-in-law.

The two younger women now looked at each other and embraced.

"I'm so happy, Jessica, I truly am," Iris said, her eyes bright with tears. "And it's not only because marrying Eric will solve so many of our problems. Just think, we won't have to skimp and watch every penny now, and I'll be able to take Mother off your hands. But I also think I'm actually in love. I know I am!" she added with emphasis.

"I know it, too," Jessica said, her own eyes filling with tears. "You couldn't spend five minutes, let alone a lifetime, with a man you didn't care for."

Iris gave her another hug and declared, "I'm going to spoil him, and he's going to spoil me, and we're going to be divinely happy."

"I know," Jessica said again. "And it couldn't happen to a more wonderful woman."

Iris grew suddenly sober. "Yes, it could. It could happen to *you,* darling. Don't look at me like that, now, I know what I'm saying. You and Roderick had something wonderful and rare, but you can't live on the memory of that for the rest of your life."

The past twenty-four hours flashed through Jessica's mind, and she turned away. But Iris didn't notice. "You've got to have more in your life than just battling through it day by day. If it hadn't been for you, Mother and I... well, we would have just gone under.... I can't think what would have become of us. No, don't look like that, it's true. But now that I'm going to marry Eric, you'll be free. You can do something for yourself for a change."

"What do you suggest?" Jessica asked, trying to keep her tone light.

"To begin with, you could let yourself fall in love," Iris suggested seriously.

"Let myself—" Jessica began incredulously, but was interrupted.

Beyond Pride

"Don't pretend you're thick, dear, you know exactly what I mean—and with whom."

"I can't imagine what—"

"Then let me spell it out," Iris offered, looking at her levelly. "With Peter Savage, the man you could love if you let yourself. The man who is in love with you. What could be more perfect?"

"What, indeed?" Jessica joked to hide her confusion. "A perfect way to get to live in Romney House again."

"Don't waste sarcasm on me." Iris waved at her airily. "You know I'm immune to it. The fact that he owns Romney House has nothing to do with it—though I will admit it's rather a divine coincidence. But it wouldn't matter if the chap lived in a tin shed. He'd still be the right one for you."

"When did you decide this?" Jessica demanded in an outraged voice.

"When I first became aware of those currents passing between you two. I would have had to be three months dead and buried not to have noticed them."

"Currents passing between..." Jessica repeated and shuddered with a grimace of distaste. "Why, Iris, that ghastly cliché can only be from one of your dreadful plays."

Musingly, Iris put a thoughtful finger to her lips. "I believe it *is* from something I once appeared in," she admitted, unabashed, "though I can't remember *which* dreadful play. However, it happens to fill the bill in this case. I sensed it that first evening he walked in here and sprang his little surprise on us, and it's been obvious ever since that he's head over heels in love with you—as you could be with him if you'd only let yourself."

"I didn't know so many hackneyed phrases could be packed into one sentence." Jessica laughed a little lamely, trying to hide the disturbing effect of Iris's words.

Iris shrugged, unoffended. "Love is the most hackneyed thing in the world. Look at me, I've been in and out of it since I was ten years old. The trick is to recognize the real thing from all the trial runs. I have. Think you can?" she challenged.

Jessica glanced away from Iris's too frank gaze. Under the circumstances, her words were inflicting painful little wounds. "I think your brain has become fogged by romance. It's a known condition of all newly engaged women that they immediately try to pair everyone else off," she accused her jokingly.

"Well, all right, have it your way. Go on fooling yourself, as long as you don't think you're fooling *me,*" Iris said. With a significant parting look, she left the room.

Jessica sat down on the chaise by her window and looked out into the darkness. No lights burned in the distant mansion. The night before, when she had sat looking out into the darkness like this, now seemed a lifetime away.

Iris's words ran insistently through her head, but everything that had happened between her and Peter Savage that morning denied their truth. Head over heels in love, indeed! But as she sat there, her eyes kept stealing back to Romney House, hoping to see a light come on there.

When she finally went downstairs to join the others, Carlotta and Iris were already in the middle of drawing up lavish plans for the forthcoming wedding. It was to be the biggest splash Sommerville had seen in a long time, a double celebration, partly for the nuptials, partly as a sort of comeback for the Romneys. Eric, who wasn't averse to a little pomp and fuss centered around his person, concurred willingly with everything. It was agreed that the engagement would be sprung as a surprise at a dinner party at the end of the following week. Until then it was to remain a secret from everyone but Eric's parents. Jessica hadn't seen Iris and Carlotta so happy and excited for a long time. When she finally staggered off to bed, she was so totally exhausted that for the first time in her life she lay down in her clothes and immediately fell into a deep sleep.

* * *

The next morning, thickheaded and dizzy, she padded into the bathroom and took a cold shower. Looking down at her thigh she saw that the skin had been scraped and that there were long scratch marks. She must have hurt herself when she clambered up the rock after her midnight swim. With a devastating rush, every vivid detail of that night came back to her. Despite all that had happened since then she realized with surprise that she didn't regret a moment of it.

The house was silent, the others still asleep after their late night, when she went down to make coffee. She almost dropped her cup when the phone rang. Her hands weren't quite steady as she answered it, and she had to keep the disappointment from her voice when Eric's mother identified herself on the other end. She was overcome with delight, having just heard the news from her son that moment. Keeping Jessica on the phone for almost twenty minutes with her outpourings of joy over this unexpected development, she finally hung up with the promise that she'd be there soon.

Gwen Cuttler arrived a little after lunch and immediately plunged with gusto into the great campaign. First they planned the small dinner party at which the engagement was to be announced. Twenty guests were decided on, local friends such as the Phillipses and Marjorie Cunningham as well as some of the Cuttlerses' Sydney relatives.

"And Peter Savage, of course—we mustn't leave him out," Iris said with a mischievous glance at Jessica.

"No!" Jessica exclaimed in a tone that made everyone in the room look at her in surprise. "I mean," she stammered, wilting under their stares, "I don't think he'll be here. I seem to remember he mentioned some plans he had in Sydney at that time. Something to do with a new building..." Her voice trailed off as she met Iris's speculative stare. As soon as she could, she made an excuse and escaped into the garden. Disregarding the unsuitability of her clothes, she got down on her hands and knees and began furiously to weed one of the flower beds.

For a moment the idea of inviting him after all was tempting. How satisfying to see his face when the engagement was announced! It would have been sweet revenge to witness his reaction to the facts. But no, she decided, her first impulse not to invite him had been right after all. She was through playing games. Somehow she always seemed to come out the loser. Besides, he would hear soon enough.

While her hands were busy with the task of pulling out weeds, she considered the future. With a pang she realized how much she would miss Iris. Despite their differences they had been close friends from the first. Iris had a brazen, if irresponsible, attitude toward life, an unshakable cheerfulness that had helped lighten their darkest days. This marriage was the best thing that could have happened to her. Her future, as Peter Savage had painted it, would otherwise have been rather bleak. Again Jessica admitted that Peter had been right.

Jessica also considered the difference the marriage would make to her own life. Her responsibilities would certainly be lighter, but they wouldn't be over as far as Carlotta was concerned. No doubt she would spend a lot of time with her daughter and son-in-law, but her permanent home would still be with Jessica. Eric's business involved frequent travel, and she guessed the newlyweds would be away a great deal. She and Carlotta would continue together in their little cottage.

For her own part, accepting any financial assistance from her future brother-in-law was out of the question. More and more in the past weeks she had been growing restless and becoming strongly attracted to the idea of pursuing some sort of career. She would have to think it over very carefully.

The garden gate gave its familiar squeak, and she looked up to see Marjorie Cunningham hurrying up the path. Spotting Jessica, Marjorie gave a wave and came over.

"Hello, Jessica dear, I heard the Cuttlers were back in town. I came over to see if you would all like to have dinner with me tonight."

"Everyone's inside. Come on, I'll walk back with you," Jessica said, leading the way to the drawing room, where the conference was taking place.

"Hello, what's going on?" Marjorie asked with interest when she saw Iris, Eric, Gwen, and Carlotta bent conspiratorially over the table. "Planning something?" she inquired curiously.

Iris raised her eyes to the ceiling.

"Only a dinner party for Saturday night. Of course, you're invited," Iris told her.

"Oh, lovely," Marjorie exclaimed, her suspicions that they were planning some charity function without her knowledge put to rest. "What's the occasion?"

"You'll find out at the party, dear," Carlotta said with an air of deliberate mystery.

Instantly Marjorie's suspicions were on the alert again. She looked at the smugly smiling faces of the group and her eyes roamed about trying to find a clue to their behavior. Suddenly they lit on Iris's left hand, and she let out a scream of surprise. "Iris! Is that an engagement ring?"

Iris appeared half annoyed and half pleased that her surprise had been sprung. "It certainly is," she said, flashing it triumphantly.

Marjorie's eyes goggled at this unexpected news. "Iris, I had no idea! Who is it?"

"Me," Eric said proudly, putting an arm around his fiancée.

At this Marjorie's jaw dropped open, and it was a few seconds before she could stammer, "You two? But I never dreamt..."

"Don't feel bad, Marjorie." Iris was tickled, knowing how hard Marjorie worked at always knowing everything. "No one dreamt it. It even came as a surprise to Eric and me, didn't it, darling?"

It was a full half hour and several cups of tea later that Marjorie was finally able to digest the news. After a lengthy visit, she finally took her leave.

"Remember," Iris called, "it's supposed to be a surprise, so for goodness' sake don't blab."

Marjorie turned back indignantly. "Really, Iris, you know I'm not in the habit of gossiping!"

"I don't know anything of the sort," Iris retorted. "And by the way," she called with elaborate innocence, "would you like to bring an escort on Saturday? What about that distinguished-looking gentleman you've been seeing so much of— what's his name? Charlie somebody, I think."

Marjorie flushed an unbecoming scarlet. "That won't be necessary, thank you," she said stiffly.

Jessica felt a sudden sympathy for her and tactfully broached the subject again as she walked her to the gate. "Why don't you take Iris at her word and bring Charlie? He's such a charming man, I'm sure it'll be fun to have him."

Marjorie gave her a covert glance, then drew herself straighter and patted her hair in a fluttery gesture. "Well, he has been rather attentive, and I've been his guest at dinner once or twice. Perhaps I ought to invite him...just as a courtesy, you know. Yes, I believe I will. Tell Iris for me, will you?" Her steps took on a new sprightliness as she walked to her car.

"It'll be a pleasure," Jessica called after her.

There was romance in the air everywhere, she thought wistfully as she walked back to the house. How Peter would have enjoyed hearing of this latest progress between his friend and the town's resident snob.

With sudden truthfulness she admitted to herself how much she had wanted to hear from him since her return yesterday, how she had waited for every ring of the telephone, every knock on the door.

The engagement party was still days away. Perhaps she wouldn't hear from him until after that. Impatiently she fixed all her hopes on that time.

chapter 13

DURING THE NEXT few days of restless longing, followed by endless, sleepless nights, Jessica tried to pinpoint the exact moment when she had fallen in love with Peter Savage. For she could no longer ignore the truth. She wasn't even sure she wanted to. Now it seemed she had known it deep down for a long time.

Time and again she went over every meeting, every word, every gesture they had exchanged. Time and again she relived the night at his beach house. But she couldn't come up with the answer she sought. Falling in love, she decided, had no beginning—that was why it was called "falling." All of a sudden, before you realized it, you were there, captive. Once you did realize it, it seemed the knowledge had been there all the time.

She tried to comfort herself with the thought that, once Peter learned of Iris's engagement, she would hear from him, but that didn't make the intervening days any easier to bear. And while waiting impatiently, she suffered through a confusing range of emotions—from anger to dejection to hope. Sometimes she decided he cared for her, too—she had only to remember that night to be certain of it—but then she remembered his cruel words and was certain he didn't care at all.

On the morning of the engagement party, she sat polishing silver in the dining room in an angry, resentful mood. What sheer callousness and indifference not to have called all this time. He was probably busy, surrounded by a flock of women somewhere while she was eating her heart out over him. If and when he did show up, she would have a few things to say to him! She took her anger out on a sterling sugar bowl and gave it the polishing of its life.

All around her the house rang with voices. Sooner than she would have believed possible, the Romney household had been thrown into a fever of turmoil. And the engagement hadn't even been announced yet! The frenzy of planning had grown into an orgy of list writing—lists for trousseaus, lists for the florist, lists of linen and silver patterns, lists of menus, lists of ideal honeymoon spots, lists of parties and of people to invite to them. Iris and Carlotta were fully indulging themselves in an excitement that had been long denied them.

Eric was always there, his mother was there most of the time, and Marjorie, anxious to miss nothing, popped in several times a day. Even sensible, practical Mrs. Green succumbed to the fever of excitement. At times it seemed to Jessica that she was the only sane one in the place. Everyone came to her for advice or approval, and she was kept busy helping out in addition to keeping up with her usual duties.

She had finished with the silver bowl and was polishing a cake stand when Iris and Carlotta returned from town and popped in to show off their new hairdos.

"Will you look at her, Mother," Iris exclaimed. "Up to her elbows in grimy work while us wicked stepsisters and stepmothers are preening ourselves for the ball. Well, you know how *that* story ends." Hustling her confused mother out of the room, she turned back and told Jessica with a sly grin, "Remember, Cinderella dear, it wasn't *my* idea to leave Prince Charming off the guest list." She scurried outside to escape the polishing cloth that came sailing in her direction.

Some time later, Jessica had almost finished when Mrs. Green's head popped around the door. "That nice young bloke here to see you love," she bawled. "Says he wants to talk to you alone."

Beyond Pride 167

Jessica's heart leaped into her throat. There could be only one "nice young bloke," and she felt both weak with happiness and shakily unnerved by his arrival.

Her trembling hands fumbled awkwardly to free themselves of the stained rubber gloves she was wearing. In a moment she was out of the room and up the stairs. She rushed to the bathroom to wash her hands, tore off the overalls she had worn to protect her dress, and hurried to the mirror. Her face was flushed, her eyes dilated. Even her hair seemed to be suffering from shock.

Jessica's resentment, her desire to give Peter a piece of her mind, were forgotten. He must have come because he'd heard of the engagement and wanted to apologize. Now that he was here, waiting to see her, it didn't even matter that he had said those terrible things to her. She could even feel glad that he had been jealous of Eric. When she went downstairs she would go straight to him, and everything would be as it had been the night they had made love.

Trembling with anticipation, she gave her hair a quick brushing and put some powder and fresh lipstick on, then, head bowed, leaned on the dressing table for support. She waited until she ws calm enough to assume at least a pretense at composure. At last she was ready.

He was standing on the brick path he had laid out not so long before, his back turned to the house. Jessica stood still for a moment, overwhelmed by the sheer joy of seeing him before her. The little composure she had mustered upstairs deserted her. Her face lit with happy anticipation, and she took a few steps toward him.

At the sound of her approach, he whirled around. A single glance at his face made her heart take a sickening plunge, and her smile faded. His face was ashen with barely suppressed rage, and his eyes bored into hers with cold contempt.

He looked her up and down, as if fighting to gain control of himself before daring to speak. When at last he did, his words came from between clenched teeth.

"Tell me just one thing, Mrs. Romney. Were you

already engaged to Eric Cuttler when you decided to spend the night with me, or did you make the arrangements immediately after?"

Something was terribly wrong. She didn't understand! She couldn't take in what he was saying, could only understand that his eyes were filled with hatred.

"I see from your expression that you didn't intend for your little secret to leak out yet," he went on without giving her time to recover. "Though why it should be a secret I can't imagine, since I must be the only bloody fool who wasn't in on it. I still wouldn't be if not for the great luck of running into Miss Cunningham a while back. Oh, don't worry," he said in response to her sudden intake of breath, "she was as coy about the whole thing as all get-out. Said it was a big secret and she couldn't tell me too much yet. But she could barely contain herself at the wonderful news over here and dropped enough hints for me to understand—understand all too well!"

Relief flooded through Jessica. So that was it! The silly woman couldn't keep the secret to herself after all, but had fooled herself into thinking she hadn't revealed all of it. Instead, she'd done the worst thing of all by hinting at half-truths. Which had been enough to confirm Peter's suspicions—suspicions, Jessica thought with a silent curse, she had deliberately planted herself. But now that she knew the cause of his anger, she could put everything right in a few words. Her relief showed itself in a smile, but before she could speak he had turned on her again.

"I can see you find me amusing. It must have struck you wildly funny the other night when we were discussing your future and I showed such concern. All the time I was praising that gutsy exterior, the heart of a little schemer was beating underneath. I must have hit the nail right on the head when I asked whether you'd marry a man for his money. No wonder you looked so put out. All the time you had your future well in hand, didn't you, with that pompous, pathetic fool who must be too damn thick to know he's being taken for a ride!"

Beyond Pride

His words washed over Jessica in great waves of pain. Every time she tried to interrupt to stop their bitter flow and to explain, he made some new, terrible accusation that left her speechless. But when he said this last, she finally cried out, "You mustn't...you have no reason to say things like that to me!" The deathly pallor of her face matched his.

Something in him snapped. "The hell I haven't!" he said savagely, smashing his fist into the trunk of a nearby tree. "Unless you can look at me and tell me you're in love with him. Are you?" He stood over her, tense and threatening.

"I've never said that...I never said I loved him," she said quietly, her eyes holding a plea.

He flashed her a look of disgust and began pacing restlessly. Beneath his rage, beneath the ugly words, she thought she saw a hint of the pain that was fueling his anger. This was wrong, terribly, frighteningly wrong. She wanted to go to him, to stop his pacing with an embrace, to explain everything, but again he didn't give her a chance to speak, turning on her with fresh bitterness.

"Of course I should be the last to accuse Cuttler of stupidity, having been taken in so completely myself." He gave a laugh that was more bitter than his words had been. "Can you believe it, at first I even had the vanity to think you were parading him under my nose to put me in my place, or make me jealous, or whatever the hell game it is you women play. Not too bloody smart, am I? You'd hardly waste your time on foolishness like that when you had your sights set on restoring the Romneys to their former glory. That's what you want from him, isn't it? That's why you need his money! Have I hit the nail on the bloody head again?" he demanded and when, still unable to reply, she stood staring at him, he stepped closer and added brutally, "Did you go on a midnight swim with him too, or was a simple pat on the head enough for the poor boy?"

With these last words Jessica thought they had reached

the point of no return. She could have forgotten everything before now. But this was unforgivable, this was something she could never forget. The pride that she had kept suppressed through his cruel barrage now rose in her again, and the pleading look disappeared from her eyes.

Yet even as she forced herself to return his cold, unyielding stare, she was fully aware of how totally, how helplessly she loved him.

Her silence only increased his fury. Suddenly he reached out and took her arms in a crushing grip. "Don't you have something to say, Mrs. Romney?"

Jessica gave a faint shake of her head as she looked up at him. Her lips felt stiff as she spoke. "You haven't left anything for me to say. If that's how you feel—if that's what you think of me, there *is* no more to say."

He gave her a desperate look and thrust her so violently from him that she staggered backward. He resumed his frantic pacing back and forth on the same few feet of garden path. Jessica stood crushed, unable to move under the weight of this new unhappiness—such a different outcome of the meeting she had impatiently anticipated for days.

Finally he stopped pacing and straightened up as if coming to some sort of decision. His face was still pale, but it had become a rigidly controlled, cold mask.

"If you're prepared to marry someone for his money, if it's so important to you... I'll marry you."

Jessica stood stunned by this second great shock. She'd thought nothing could have equaled the first blow, but this had done it. A part of her detached itself from the rest and wondered if it was looking on some crazy, confused, distorted dream. Her hand flew to her head as if trying to clear it, and she asked in a barely audible whisper, "What... what did you say?"

"It's Romney House you really want back, isn't it? I have Romney House. So wouldn't it be smarter to marry me instead of Cuttler?" The harsh cruelty of his voice was an incongruous contrast to the marriage proposal he was making.

"I don't understand," Jessica stammered, still struggling to make sense of his words.

"I'm proposing marriage to you," he explained grimly. "I'm offering you Romney House and quite a lot of money that goes with it. Now that's not hard to understand for a shrewd little woman like you, is it?"

"Yes... yes, it is hard. In fact it's impossible to understand," she recovered enough to reply. "For the past half hour you've been telling me how much you despise me, how low your opinion is of me, and now you say you're proposing marriage to me? Yes, that is completely beyond my understanding!" Her voice rose with hysteria.

"Do you enjoy drawing this out?" he sneered. "You don't expect one of those sentimental hand-on-heart proposals, do you? Think of it as a business proposition. I think that's more in the range of your understanding. I believe I've made you an offer even Cuttler can't top."

Jessica stared at him, trying to find even the faintest resemblance in him to the man with whom she had spent one of the loveliest nights of her life. There was none. This man was a stranger, and the proposal he was making wasn't the declaration of love she had longed for. It was a horrible, deliberate insult.

It required every ounce of will to keep her voice from breaking. "Yes, it sounds like an irresistible offer," she agreed bitterly, "but I'm curious to know why you made it. Oh, I can see what's in it for *me* clearly enough, but I want to know—strictly from a business point of view, mind you—what you can possibly get out of it."

He looked away, his eyes fixed on something in the distance, while Jessica caught her breath and waited for his answer. Despite everything, a desperate hope stirred in her heart. When he looked back at her, the cold mask of his face hadn't cracked.

"I want you. I've never made a secret of that."

Jessica let out the breath she had been holding with

a sigh. It wasn't the answer she'd been waiting for. The emphasis he'd put on "want" had a debasing quality to it.

"Want me enough to marry me even though you despise me?"

"Yes, I want you enough to marry you."

"Even though you believe I'm a fortune-hunting schemer?"

The muscles of his jaw tightened. "Yes."

"Knowing that I'd accept only to get back Romney House?" she drove on recklessly.

"Yes!" The word broke from him like a curse, and he pulled her roughly to him to silence her with a kiss that was a gesture of rage, not of love.

Jessica fought free and pushed him away. "Don't you think your motives for marriage are as detestable as the ones you've accused me of?"

"At least I'm honest about them," he returned cruelly.

Jessica clenched her fists, knowing she couldn't hold back the tears much longer. "Yes, I can't accuse you of dishonesty. You've never left me in any doubt about why you... *wanted* me." She spat out the word with disgust.

He took a step toward her, and his expression altered for a brief moment. "You're wrong, so wrong about—" He stopped abruptly, the moment of weakness gone. "Wasn't it *you* who put the whole thing on that footing? Can you recall your words on the subject? I can!" He paced about again before resuming. "Why don't you just be practical about this? I'm offering you everything you want. You're not going to turn me down just because I didn't pretty up the words for you, are you?" he asked with a cold laugh.

In an instant the last of her self-control would be gone. Jessica drew on the pride that had always seen her through.

"You're offering me *nothing* I want, not one thing," she cried. "And I'm turning you down for only one reason, because... because I hate you!" she half sobbed, her heart achingly denying the words even as she spoke them.

He stood looking at her for a moment, his expression so terrible that she found it harder to endure than anything else that had happened.

"In that case, here's an engagement present from me to you," he said, and, wrenching her to him, he crushed his mouth down on hers. His hands slid over her body as if they were burning his claim on it before he roughly pushed her away from him.

"Give my best to the lucky man," he said and turned on his heel.

As Jessica watched his retreating back, sudden terror enveloped her. He was going out of her life, and this time he wouldn't come back. Nothing counted, nothing else mattered as much as that he was leaving a terrible, aching void that she knew nothing and no one would be able to fill.

"Peter!" she called after him. "Peter, please wait!" She ran to the gate in time to see his Jeep disappearing down the road.

Hours later, she was woodenly preparing for the party, as she had done everything else since he'd left. The evening stretched before her like a horrible, punishing endurance test. Suddenly she didn't think she could face it—or another moment—without seeing him. She looked toward Romney House, and like a signal a light came on in one of the upstairs windows.

In a moment she had made her decision. She threw down the brush she had been holding, stepped into the first pair of shoes that came underfoot, and rushed down the stairs and out of the house.

In the few minutes it took to drive through the twisting back road to Romney House, she made up her mind that this time nothing would stop her from speaking and explaining everything. This time *she* wouldn't let him speak until everything she'd come to say had been said. The wound to her pride could be mended later, after the wound to her heart had been tended.

She arrived outside the mansion's closed gate and sounded her horn impatiently.

After what seemed like a torturous eternity, Mr. Curtis, the gardener, came shuffling to the gate and peered out at her.

"That Mrs. Romney, is it? Evening," he greeted.

"Hello, Mr. Curtis, I'd like to see Mr. Savage, please." Jessica forced herself to be courteous despite an impulse to crash the car through the gates.

"Ah well, afraid he's not here, Mrs. Romney. Asked me to move in for a while to keep an eye on the place for him. Went away a while ago, said he didn't know when he would be back again."

A sick feeling tore through Jessica, and she bowed her head over the steering wheel.

chapter 14

JESSICA REINED IN the chestnut mare and with a light, graceful swing lowered herself from the saddle. The mare's polished skin glistened with sweat, and her breath rasped with the exertion of the spirited ride they had just ended.

"Sorry, Molly, hope I wasn't too hard on you," Jessica murmured, running her hand over the beautiful, white-starred forehead. The horse gave her a velvety side glance from enormous, long-fringed brown eyes, twitched her ears, and began to browse peacefully in the grass at her feet.

Jessica sank to the ground, leaning her back against the trunk of a tree. The morning's wild gallop was one of many similarly vigorous activities she had thrown herself into in the past couple of weeks. She was brimming over with a desperate, restless energy for which she sought outlets in fierce games of tennis, golf, swimming, and riding. She couldn't allow herself to keep still for long, because then she would begin to think, and the pain would come again.

Time had not shown the least inclination to perform those healing miracles with which it was always being credited. To keep herself from succumbing to the desolation in her heart, Jessica forced herself to the limits of physical exertion. Only then could she fall asleep, exhausted, but she always awoke too early to a terrible, aching emptiness.

She jumped up restlessly again and climbed a rock to look around her. She had come to the quarry, a place she had visited several times in the past two weeks. She was haunting all the places where she and Peter had been together. She had even driven past the Royal Victoria, though her pride had not allowed her to go inside to inquire after its owner. She didn't really expect to see Peter in any of these places, but she found comfort in going to them, as if his presence still lingered there.

Everyone in Sommerville had remarked on the sudden, unexpected disappearance of Peter Savage. It was odd, they remarked, that just when he appeared to be settling in, he went away. Right in the middle of the busiest social season of the year, too, when several Christmas parties were being given. He hadn't spoken to anyone of his plans, had said good-bye to no one, had only told the caretaker of his house that he didn't know when he would be back. Jessica said nothing, even when Iris tried to question her. She couldn't bear to talk about Peter Savage.

She had returned home after going to Romney House to hear of his departure and had gone through the motions of hosting the engagement party. She prided herself now on having given a very credible performance. The party had been a great success, and everyone had been gratifyingly surprised and delighted at the announcement. But Jessica had found it painfully ironic to sit there with a smile plastered on her face when a few hours before she had turned down a proposal herself.

At first Jessica could barely bring herself to be civil to Marjorie. If not for the silly woman's tattle, her whole life might have been different, she thought savagely. But she knew that what had happened between Peter and her was not in the least Marjorie's fault. It was her own perverse pride that had prevented her from telling him the truth.

Spurred on by sudden anger at herself, Jessica mounted Molly again and galloped all the way to the

Phillips farm. Once she had unsaddled and wiped down the horse—one of many in the Phillips stables—she drove home.

The front door of the cottage stood open, and she heard the sound of laughter from inside. She hurried through the hall into the drawing room.

Iris and Carlotta had spent the past three days shopping in Sydney. The drawing room was a chaos of parcels, wrapping paper, and spilling boxes. Every surface in the room seemed draped with frothy, lacy lingerie, stockings, scarves, blouses, skirts, and dresses.

"I see you've bought a few badly needed rags," Jessica remarked dryly, looking about the messy room and thinking of Iris's already bursting closets upstairs.

"Jessie, Mother and I have found the most divine things," Iris squealed excitedly, holding up a pale green negligee in one hand and a gold lamé hostess gown in the other. "We did all our Christmas shopping, too. Eric has already opened accounts for me in the most wonderful little shops in the city, and I just went crazy. Wait till you see the beautiful Christmas present I bought for you. You're going to die!"

"I think Eric's death will precede mine when he sees the bills," Jessica predicted.

"Oh, I don't know, not if I'm wearing *this* when I show them to him." Iris smirked, holding up a gossamer nightgown with a deeply plunging neckline.

"Iris, really! You're too crass for words," Carlotta chided in a shocked voice.

"I can afford to be broad-minded, Mother. I'm an engaged woman," Iris told her smugly.

Carlotta went upstairs to take a nap before dinner, leaving the two younger women alone together.

Iris turned to Jessica with a suddenly anxious expression. "Darling, are you all right? You look so...so keyed up and exhausted."

"I'm neither. I'm fine, really," she protested with a smile.

"Is that why you're making confetti of that card?" Iris asked, looking pointedly at a small heap of paper in Jessica's lap.

She glanced down and saw guiltily that she'd been demolishing one of the Christmas cards with which a small side table was decorated.

"You've got the fidgets about something, all right," Iris diagnosed, looking at her sharply. "It's so unlike you, too. Usually you're the calmest of creatures. But for the past couple of weeks—actually since you went to Sydney that time—you've been acting as if... I don't know... as if you were being driven or something. Won't you tell me what it is, dear?"

"Really, it's nothing," Jessica insisted, keeping her eyes in her lap. "There is so much happening right now— your engagement, Christmas, the wedding—I guess you're right, I'm a little keyed up over them."

"Bull," Iris said inelegantly. "I've seen you cope with ten times as much without turning a hair. Okay, don't tell me. But you know, you have a stubborn streak that's going to cause you grief some day." Her tone was unusually solemn, but in a moment she smiled again and went to put an arm about Jessica. "Otherwise you're perfect," she joked. "And as soon as this circus is over I think you should go away on a long holiday. I've been thinking that you should go back to the States for a visit. Don't worry about the financial side because I'll... Oh, is that the doorbell? I'm expecting Eric this afternoon. I guess I'd better not bring him in here," she said hesitantly, looking about the clothes-littered room. She added with a grin, "I don't want to treat him to a sneak preview." Tossing down a delicate bit of silk and lace finery, she went to the door. "I'll take him into the study."

After she left, Jessica automatically began to tidy up. She picked up the scattered pieces of Iris's trousseau and, folding them neatly, stacked them on the sofa.

Iris' mention of a trip coincided with an idea she herself had been considering for the past few days. After the wedding the house would fall into a terrible lull. She didn't think she could face the empty days. Planning a trip back to the States would give her restless mind the occupation it needed. One instant she thought it a wonderful idea and was impatient to go. The next she didn't know how she would be able to tear herself away from here for even a day. What if while she was away he... But no, she tried to put that thought from her mind. She couldn't pin her hopes on that any longer.

She didn't know if she would ever see him again. The thought that he might sell or rent Romney House and never return tormented her until an even more unbearable idea took its place. What if he did come back—but with someone else?

Iris couldn't have known how right she'd been when she'd warned Jessica that her stubbornness would cause her grief. She was paying for that stubborn pride every waking moment of the day. She saw now how much it had been responsible for their mutual antagonism from the first.

Peter had proposed to her, had been prepared to spend the rest of his life with her, but that same cursed pride had prevented her from seeing beyond his wounding words. If she had known where to find him, she would have gone to him a thousand times over, but as the days passed, it became more and more obvious that he didn't want to be found.

She picked up the sheer negligee Iris had flaunted before her mother and, with an instinctively feminine gesture, held it against her. If she hadn't been such a fool, such an obstinate damn fool, she might have been trying on her own trousseau right now.

With a caressing touch, she smoothed the weightless fabric against her body. She was still in this pose when she turned around in response to a light knock on the door.

It slowly opened, and Peter Savage stepped inside.

Jessica felt the room reel about her. Please... please don't let this be one of my wishful dreams, she prayed intensely.

He stood at the door staring wordlessly at her, then, running his fingers through his hair in an awkward gesture, took a step toward her. His eyes slid from her face to the garment she was holding against her, and she saw him stop as if jerked back by a violent hand. His eyes slowly scanned the room, taking in all the other pieces that still lay scattered about. His breath caught sharply before he turned to stare at her again.

Jessica grew weak and dizzy with a rapid succession of emotions. She was incredulous, overwhelmingly relieved, and wild with joy. She still couldn't believe he was there.

Her eyes followed his, and she quickly thrust the negligee away from her onto the table next to which she was standing.

He must have learned about Iris and Eric's engagement. But why was he looking about him as if every piece of clothing his eyes lit on gave him fresh pain?

"Hello... Peter."

"I've been away," he told her unnecessarily.

"I know," she replied, her eyes searching his face hungrily. "Can I... Would you like something to drink?" Part of her brain registered the fact that in times of crisis people reached for the nearest banality.

"Yes... no, no I don't think so, thanks," he replied distractedly. He had been staring at her steadily, and she noted with perverse satisfaction that his face looked worn with strain. He turned from her and walked over to the window, where he stood looking out.

Jessica searched for the right words with which to go to him, but, before she found them, he turned toward her again. His eyes lingered on the piles of luxurious underwear, then turned away in disgust.

Once again he ran a nervous hand through his hair before bursting out, "I've just spent the most bloody miserable two weeks of my life. How were yours?"

A great wave of joy swept all the misery of the past two weeks away from Jessica. "The worst," she told him happily.

He looked at her quickly, and she saw a flicker of hope in his eyes. "Well, then—" he began, but his eyes strayed back to the pieces of lingerie, as if he was fascinated by them against his will.

Why? Jessica asked herself again. Why was he looking at those innocent, inanimate clothes with such hatred? He tore his eyes away, and she wanted to go to him to kiss away the lines of strain from his face.

"Have you given my offer any more thought?" He tried to sound cool, but this time Jessica wasn't deterred by his tone. This time nothing would stop her. This time, no matter what, she wouldn't let him walk out of her life.

"I've thought of nothing else," she admitted, looking up at him with her heart in her eyes.

"And—" he asked hoarsely, closing the gap between them with a quick step.

This was too easy, she thought. After the days of agony it was too unbelievably easy.

"And I... accept it," she whispered.

The expression that swept over his face matched everything that was in her heart. They stood looking at each other, too overcome by the moment even to reach out or speak. He took a long, deep breath and stepped back a little to put some distance between them.

"Then the first thing you'd better do is burn all... that. Right now!" he ordered in an unsteady voice, waving his hand to include Iris's purchases. His voice was filled with pain and anger.

At first slowly, then with growing certainty, the truth dawned on her. He didn't know about the engagement! He thought all this was her own trousseau! No wonder he had looked at everything with such hatred. He thought she had bought them for her marriage with Eric. He was still convinced she was planning to marry Eric, yet he had come back to her to renew his proposal.

Jessica's happiness was boundless, her love for him overwhelming. He loved her enough to have swallowed his pride, overcome his contempt, and come back to her.

It was a few seconds before she could trust herself to speak.

"Why on earth should I burn Iris's underwear?" she cried.

"Iris's!" He stared at her uncomprehendingly.

Jessica nodded. "Eric would be furious with me. He spent a fortune on the stuff. And I don't want my future brother-in-law mad at me," she said with a broad smile.

Peter frowned, and a dangerous flame leaped into his eyes. "What damn game... What are you saying, Jessica?" he demanded.

In a few breathless, rushed words Jessica explained everything. He listened to her, incredulously at first, then with growing, painful consternation. When she finished, he let out an explosive breath and buried his head in his hands.

He began to curse himself. "What a fool, what a great, certifiable—" Abruptly he stopped, and his head shot up from his hands. His blue eyes glinted with anger as he looked at her.

"You mean you knew this all the time and didn't say a word? Not one word? You let me say all those... those awful things to you, watched me make a fool of myself and throw my pride into your lap and said *nothing?*" His voice rose to a shout. "You let us both go through two weeks of hell just because you—"

But the rest of his words were never spoken, because with one move Jessica was in his arms, her lips pressed to his. A long moment later she whispered, "I learned this method of stopping a quarrel from a good friend of mine."

"You'd better stop me some more. I'm as mad as hell," he whispered back, his mouth already covering hers.

When the first rush of intensity passed, he murmured to her again, "Love, how could you have let me say those things to you?"

"I was too hurt to stop you."

"How could I have said them?" he asked again with

bitter self-accusation. "Of course I was hurting too, you know. I was mad with jealousy, I kept telling myself you couldn't care for Cuttler, but that was small comfort to a man crazy in love—"

"A man what?" Jessica interrupted.

"You heard." He laughed, placing a light kiss on her forehead.

"Just wanted to make sure," she replied with a blissful sigh.

"Don't be coy, Jessie, you've known for a long time."

Jessica shook her head, snuggling closer into his arms. "Now that you're here I know it, and it seems I should have known all along. But if someone had asked me an hour ago..." Suddenly she drew away and faced him with some of her old spirit. "You weren't exactly the answer to a woman's dreams of romance in the beginning, you know! You played some low-down tricks and went out of your way to be unpleasant to me. What was that *Taming of the Shrew* stuff anyway?"

"I told you before." He laughed. "It was the only line I could take after you high-handedly called me 'young man.'"

"I know, I know," Jessica conceded, then added more seriously, "You never once said the word *love,* only *want.*"

"I didn't dare. But you must know how often I came close to it, don't you?"

"You didn't dare?" she asked, marveling. "You're the most daring, impertinent man I've ever met."

"You can be a pretty formidable lady yourself when you get that steely look in your eyes."

"Scared you, huh?" Jessica asked triumphantly.

It was his turn to become serious. "Falling in love like that did unnerve me. And I didn't know how else to get through that pride of yours and your independence... and the memories you held of your marriage."

The next few seconds were taken up with another lingering kiss.

"Did you believe all those horrible things about me?"

Jessica asked, pulling slightly away.

"I believed you were engaged to Cuttler, yes. Everything else came out of my anger and disappointment over that. Don't expect a jealous man to be reasonable, darling." He looked down at her, his face still serious, and said, "I love you, Jessica."

Jessica, who a minute ago had thought she had already reached the limits of happiness, went limp in his arms at this simplest but deepest declaration that can be made between two people. Her own reply was lost under a shower of kisses.

At that moment the door burst open, and Carlotta entered. "What—" she began, then stood rooted to the spot, staring at the embracing couple. Iris, who had rushed to stop her mother from intruding on them but arrived at the door too late, stood behind her.

She took one look into the room and her face lit up with joy. She took Carlotta's arm and turned her around.

"Come along, Mother. Stop gawking, now. You know how hard it is to get a decent plumber these days. Jessica's just making sure this one stays in the family."

WATCH FOR
6 NEW TITLES EVERY MONTH!

Second Chance at Love

- ___ 05703-7 **FLAMENCO NIGHTS #1** Susanna Collins
- ___ 05637-5 **WINTER LOVE SONG #2** Meredith Kingston
- ___ 05624-3 **THE CHADBOURNE LUCK #3** Lucia Curzon
- ___ 05777-0 **OUT OF A DREAM #4** Jennifer Rose
- ___ 05878-5 **GLITTER GIRL #5** Jocelyn Day
- ___ 05863-7 **AN ARTFUL LADY #6** Sabina Clark
- ___ 05694-4 **EMERALD BAY #7** Winter Ames
- ___ 05776-2 **RAPTURE REGAINED #8** Serena Alexander
- ___ 05801-7 **THE CAUTIOUS HEART #9** Philippa Heywood
- ___ 05907-2 **ALOHA YESTERDAY #10** Meredith Kingston
- ___ 05638-3 **MOONFIRE MELODY #11** Lily Bradford
- ___ 06132-8 **MEETING WITH THE PAST #12** Caroline Halter
- ___ 05623-5 **WINDS OF MORNING #13** Laurie Marath
- ___ 05704-5 **HARD TO HANDLE #14** Susanna Collins
- ___ 06067-4 **BELOVED PIRATE #15** Margie Michaels
- ___ 05978-1 **PASSION'S FLIGHT #16** Marilyn Mathieu
- ___ 05847-5 **HEART OF THE GLEN #17** Lily Bradford
- ___ 05977-3 **BIRD OF PARADISE #18** Winter Ames
- ___ 05705-3 **DESTINY'S SPELL #19** Susanna Collins
- ___ 06106-9 **GENTLE TORMENT #20** Johanna Phillips
- ___ 06059-3 **MAYAN ENCHANTMENT #21** Lila Ford
- ___ 06301-0 **LED INTO SUNLIGHT #22** Claire Evans
- ___ 06131-X **CRYSTAL FIRE #23** Valerie Nye
- ___ 06150-6 **PASSION'S GAMES #24** Meredith Kingston
- ___ 06160-3 **GIFT OF ORCHIDS #25** Patti Moore
- ___ 06108-5 **SILKEN CARESSES #26** Samantha Carroll
- ___ 06318-5 **SAPPHIRE ISLAND #27** Diane Crawford
- ___ 06335-5 **APHRODITE'S LEGEND #28** Lynn Fairfax
- ___ 06336-3 **TENDER TRIUMPH #29** Jasmine Craig
- ___ 06280-4 **AMBER-EYED MAN #30** Johanna Phillips
- ___ 06249-9 **SUMMER LACE #31** Jenny Nolan
- ___ 06305-3 **HEARTTHROB #32** Margarett McKean
- ___ 05626-X **AN ADVERSE ALLIANCE #33** Lucia Curzon
- ___ 06162-X **LURED INTO DAWN #34** Catherine Mills

Second Chance at Love

- 06195-6 **SHAMROCK SEASON #35** Jennifer Rose
- 06304-5 **HOLD FAST TIL MORNING #36** Beth Brookes
- 06282-0 **HEARTLAND #37** Lynn Fairfax
- 06408-4 **FROM THIS DAY FORWARD #38** Jolene Adams
- 05968-4 **THE WIDOW OF BATH #39** Anne Devon
- 06400-9 **CACTUS ROSE #40** Zandra Colt
- 06401-7 **PRIMITIVE SPLENDOR #41** Katherine Swinford
- 06424-6 **GARDEN OF SILVERY DELIGHTS #42** Sharon Francis
- 06521-8 **STRANGE POSSESSION #43** Johanna Phillips
- 06326-6 **CRESCENDO #44** Melinda Harris
- 05818-1 **INTRIGUING LADY #45** Daphne Woodward
- 06547-1 **RUNAWAY LOVE #46** Jasmine Craig
- 06423-8 **BITTERSWEET REVENGE #47** Kelly Adams
- 06541-2 **STARBURST #48** Tess Ewing
- 06540-4 **FROM THE TORRID PAST #49** Ann Cristy
- 06544-7 **RECKLESS LONGING #50** Daisy Logan
- 05851-3 **LOVE'S MASQUERADE #51** Lillian Marsh
- 06148-4 **THE STEELE HEART #52** Jocelyn Day
- 06422-X **UNTAMED DESIRE #53** Beth Brookes
- 06651-6 **VENUS RISING #54** Michelle Roland
- 06595-1 **SWEET VICTORY #55** Jena Hunt
- 06575-7 **TOO NEAR THE SUN #56** Aimée Duvall

All of the above titles are $1.75 per copy

Available at your local bookstore or return this form to:

SECOND CHANCE AT LOVE   Dept. BW
The Berkley/Jove Publishing Group
200 Madison Avenue, New York, New York 10016

Please enclose 75¢ for postage and handling for one book, 25¢ each add'l book ($1.50 max.). No cash, CODs or stamps. Total amount enclosed: $ _____ in check or money order.

NAME _____

ADDRESS _____

CITY _____ STATE/ZIP _____

Allow six weeks for delivery.   SK-41

Second Chance at Love

- 05625-1 **MOURNING BRIDE** #57 Lucia Curzon
- 06411-4 **THE GOLDEN TOUCH** #58 Robin James
- 06596-X **EMBRACED BY DESTINY** #59 Simone Hadary
- 06660-5 **TORN ASUNDER** #60 Ann Cristy
- 06573-0 **MIRAGE** #61 Margie Michaels
- 06650-8 **ON WINGS OF MAGIC** #62 Susanna Collins
- 05816-5 **DOUBLE DECEPTION** #63 Amanda Troy
- 06675-3 **APOLLO'S DREAM** #64 Claire Evans
- 06676-1 **SMOLDERING EMBERS** #65 Marie Charles
- 06677-X **STORMY PASSAGE** #66 Laurel Blake
- 06678-8 **HALFWAY THERE** #67 Aimée Duvall
- 06679-6 **SURPRISE ENDING** #68 Elinor Stanton
- 06680-X **THE ROGUE'S LADY** #69 Anne Devon
- 06681-8 **A FLAME TOO FIERCE** #70 Jan Mathews
- 06682-6 **SATIN AND STEELE** #71 Jaelyn Conlee
- 06683-4 **MIXED DOUBLES** #72 Meredith Kingston
- 06684-2 **RETURN ENGAGEMENT** #73 Kay Robbins
- 06685-0 **SULTRY NIGHTS** #74 Ariel Tierney
- 06686-9 **AN IMPROPER BETROTHMENT** #75 Henrietta Houston
- 06687-7 **FORSAKING ALL OTHERS** #76 LaVyrle Spencer
- 06688-5 **BEYOND PRIDE** #77 Kathleen Ash
- 06689-3 **SWEETER THAN WINE** #78 Jena Hunt
- 06690-7 **SAVAGE EDEN** #79 Diane Crawford
- 06691-5 **STORMY REUNION** #80 Jasmine Craig
- 06692-3 **THE WAYWARD WIDOW** #81 Anne Mayfield

All of the above titles are $1.75 per copy

Available at your local bookstore or return this form to:

SECOND CHANCE AT LOVE
The Berkley/Jove Publishing Group
200 Madison Avenue, New York, New York 10016

Please enclose 75¢ for postage and handling for one book, 25¢ each add'l. book ($1.50 max.). No cash, CODs or stamps. Total amount enclosed: $ _____ in check or money order.

NAME _____

ADDRESS _____

CITY _____ STATE/ZIP _____

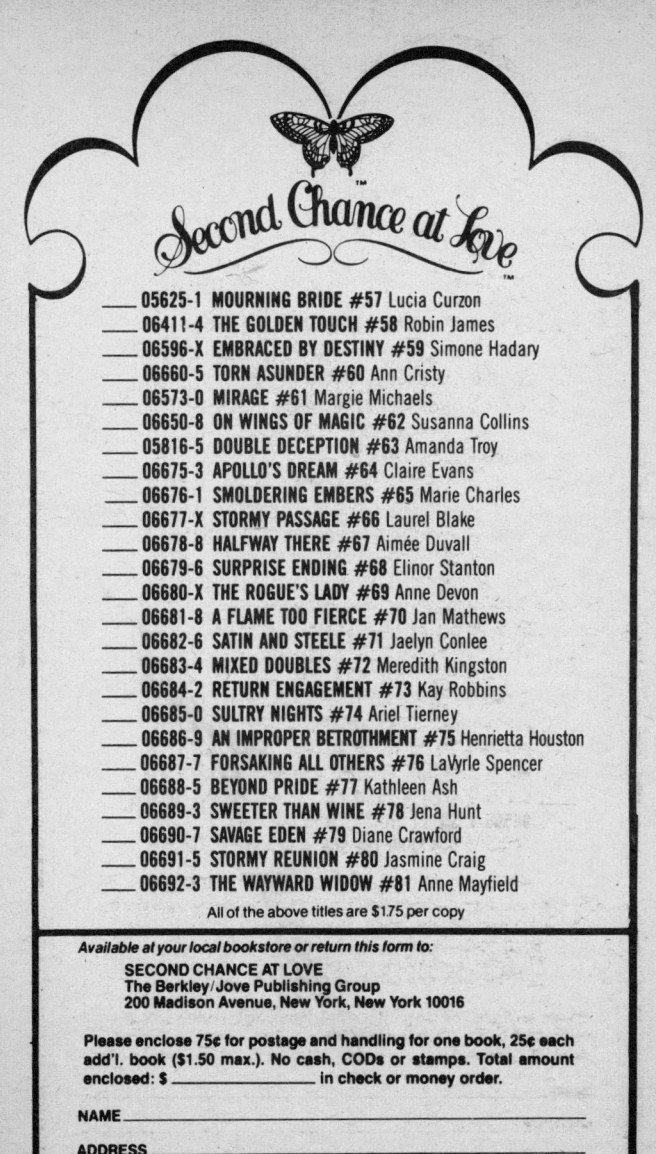

Allow six weeks for delivery.

SK-41

WHAT READERS SAY ABOUT SECOND CHANCE AT LOVE

"SECOND CHANCE AT LOVE is fantastic."
—*J. L., Greenville, South Carolina**

"SECOND CHANCE AT LOVE has all the romance of the big novels."
—*L. W., Oak Grove, Missouri**

"You deserve a standing ovation!"
—*S. C., Birch Run, Michigan**

"Thank you for putting out this type of story. Love and passion have no time limits. I look forward to more of these good books."
—*E. G., Huntsville, Alabama**

"Thank you for your excellent series of books. Our book stores receive their monthly selections between the second and third week of every month. Please believe me when I say they have a frantic female calling them every day until they get your books in."
—*C. Y., Sacramento, California**

"I have become addicted to the SECOND CHANCE AT LOVE books...You can be very proud of these books....I look forward to them each month."
—*D. A., Floral City, Florida**

"I have enjoyed every one of your SECOND CHANCE AT LOVE books. Reading them is like eating potato chips, once you start you just can't stop."
—*L. S., Kenosha, Wisconsin**

"I consider your SECOND CHANCE AT LOVE books the best on the market."
—*D. S., Redmond, Washington**

*Names and addresses available upon request